Contents

Y0-DWL-669

A Simple Christmas Story

"Wake up!" I felt my father poke me in the ribs trying to rouse me from my insensate slumber.

"Wake up, John. Don't you know what day this is?"

The sound of my father's voice so early in the morning brought back memories of my childhood when my father would wake me for an early morning fishing trip or the start of vacation. For a delicious moment I was back in my old room about to begin some adventure. Then I rolled over, opened my eyes, and, even though the room was pitch black, realized that I was back in my old room. My hand reached out for a wife who was not there.

How had I ended up here? Things had been going so well. Then the technology bubble had burst. I found myself with a wife and kids, a house that was too large, cars that were too expensive, and a stack of bills. Marriage had descended to one argument after another. We were arguing over the frustrations of life, but somehow we had become each other's target of convenience. The arguments continued until we found ourselves arguing over Christmas. The night before, Christmas Eve, I had said some things that had cut too deeply. After every other argument we had managed to get into bed and hold on to each other. This time was different. Cynthia went to the bedroom and slammed the door shut. I did not know how to take it back so I went for a drive. Somehow that drive ended up at my father's house.

I had started to sit up, but as the memory of the argument with Cynthia came back I was overwhelmed by a feeling of defeat. I rolled over and pulled up the covers. There, facing me, was the clock radio, the only light in the room. It was four am.

"Dad, don't you know what time it is?"

"It is never too late. I didn't ask any questions when you showed up here last night."

"And you shouldn't ask any now. It's too early. I don't want to talk about it. I just want to get some sleep. If you have to lecture me I'll sit still for it in the morning, but not now."

Then there was silence. I listened for the sounds of my father leaving the room. There were none. I waited with the clock radio marking the minutes. Finally, I rolled over to see if he had left. The room was too dark. His voice, low and even, came out of the dark.

"Son, it is not like that. I wanted to tell you a story, something I have never told anyone, my Christmas story."

His Christmas story. I was now wide awake. I had always regarded my father to be crazy where Christmas was concerned. In January he was already planning his Christmas decorations for the next year. All year round he would hum Christmas carols. He could not wait for Thanksgiving Day so that he could start on Christmas. No one could have had more joy out of buying a Christmas tree than my father. Decorating the tree was a celebration in itself. On Christmas day I always felt like the luckiest kid alive. My father kept up the Christmas celebration until New Years when he would start planning for the next Christmas.

Up until the time I was ten I had as much fun at Christmas as my dad. As a teenager I thought my father's behavior funny, touching, and somewhat embarrassing. When my father kept up his Christmas craziness after my two sisters and I left I thought it was his way of keeping the memories of his family alive. Then, last year, my mother became ill and died a few weeks before Christmas. My father was worn out both emotionally and physically. At the funeral strangers told me how much they would miss my mother. So many had a story of something my father did to make Christmas a little better for them or someone they knew. It made me wonder whether there was more to my father's Christmas compulsion. Last Christmas arrived and found my father's house dark. My heart broke for things passed.

Last night when I arrived the house glowed with my father's old flare. Inside a tree was decked in splendor. But I was in no mood for joy. I waved to my father, explained that I needed a place to sleep, and headed to the darkness of my old room.

"It was 1964," he began. "My father had died over a year before and left me in control of the business. I was too young and too inexperienced. Somehow I managed to hold things together without firing anybody during that first year.

"I had been working on a client for six months. This client's business would ensure the success of our business for the next year. For some reason the client called me and wanted to meet the day before Christmas to finalize our deal. I could hardly refuse. In fact, I was overjoyed at the thought of such a Christmas present.

"The client arrived at noon. We spent several hours reading through the contract, making adjustments here and there. After we had both signed I asked him to join our Christmas Eve office party. The festivities had already begun, but all eyes turned toward us as we emerged from my office. The smile on my face was enough to let everyone know how things had worked out. People who had been in fear of losing their jobs now had something to celebrate. And I, who had feared destroying in one year what my father had spent over thirty years creating, could relax.

Perhaps we partied too hard, but it seemed that there was a lot to celebrate that Christmas. The spiked punch flowed and we all got a little carried away. The time drew late. My employees left for their homes and families leaving me alone with my client. He asked if I would join him for dinner. I didn't hesitate. His faith in me would ensure the success of my company in the coming years. I thought he deserved the courtesy of the evening.

"We went to dinner at a restaurant near the office. There were drinks and wine. I was pretty high by the time I dropped him at his hotel. I remembered the presents I had left at the office and ordered the taxi driver to go there first.

"When I got to the office I was surprised to find the light on in my outer office. When I got in there I found Maxine, my secretary. Now Maxie was a few years younger than me and very attractive. This was the era of mini-skirts and the beginning of sexual liberation. Maxie flirted with me and I flirted with her. I don't think either of us wanted anything more than that.

"It turned out that Maxie was there for the same reason I was. She had gone out with a couple of girls from the office and had come back to pick up a Christmas present for her nephew. She was sloshed. Suddenly she looked at me as if I was some tasty morsel, said something about getting her Christmas present, and kissed me. Now I cared about Maxie, but I think it was more ego than anything else that made me kiss her back. That was some kiss.

"Somehow we managed to break it off. There was a little embarrassment as we collected our packages and locked up the office. On the sidewalk we gave each other a little peck on the cheek before I put her in my cab. I gave the driver enough to cover the fare and headed for the train station. The packages were not heavy and it had started to snow. I always liked walking in the snow.

"The train ride out of town went by in a haze. I was feeling pretty good about myself. It was Christmas. I had presents for the family. I was a success. I was feeling pretty good from all the drinks I had. And I had kissed a beautiful woman. Yeah, I felt pretty good.

"The time on the train sobered me up enough so I could drive home. The snow had emptied the street so I didn't see another car on the way. When I arrived home I thought I was too sober. I dropped the presents in the hall, headed for the kitchen, and poured myself another drink. After downing it I poured another and wandered out to the living room.

"The living room was dark. There, next to an undecorated tree, sat your mother.

"'Where have you been?' she said. She didn't really wait for an answer. 'The kids waited and waited for you to decorate the tree. And you didn't call. And the office didn't answer when I called. I didn't know what to think.'

"I could hear the tears in her voice. It had been a rough year. I had worked nights and weekends. When I was home I was in a bad mood. At night I didn't sleep. Your mother was left alone with two small children. I was so worried about becoming a success that I hadn't given a thought to how it was affecting my family. That night was no different. I tossed back the rest of the drink and pulled her from her chair.

"'All our problems are over. I landed the big account,' I told her.

"I wrapped my arms around her and tried to kiss her. She wouldn't let me kiss her. She squirmed this way and that. I tried to hold her tighter and tighter.

"'Come on. Give me a kiss,' I said.

"'No! Your too drunk and I'm too angry,' she returned.

"She ran into the kitchen where the light was on. I followed and made another attempt to hold her. She slipped away. Taking a look at me in the light her eyes went wide and she slapped me. When I recovered we stared at each other. It couldn't have been very long. It seemed to last forever. At last, without either of us saying a word she ran out of the room, up the stairs, and slammed the door to our bedroom.

"Jan, dear Jan. I never got tired of seeing her smile, but that night the look on her face was frightening. I think the slap in the face had been more of a shock to her than to me. I didn't blame her for that. I kept asking myself how could I have hurt the one I love so much? What had I done?

"I went into the bathroom to wash up. I looked into the mirror and there it was, lipstick. How could I have been such a fool? I threw a towel against the wall, grabbed my hat and coat, and stormed out of the house.

"There were still a few flurries in the air. Most of the town was covered by a blanket of new snow. The only marks were the tire tracks I had made driving home. As I said before, I always enjoyed walking in the snow. I buttoned up my coat and headed into town on foot.

"The town didn't amount to much in those days, just the railroad station and a few blocks of stores in each direction. Still, the city fathers tried to make it look nice for Christmas. They had wreaths hanging from every streetlight. The library and railroad station had nicely decorated trees in front. And City Hall had "Noel" spelled out in lights. I wandered around town looking at the decorations in the store windows until I noted the old church. There was a lighted nativity scene on its lawn. I walked over and right up onto the lawn to look it over. There were sheep and goats. They had shepherds and wise men. When I got to the manger I kneeled down to take a closer look at the baby. The manger was filled with snow. I gently brushed it away. I leaned over to blow the last flakes away so I could see the face. Then the lights went out.

"I got up and walked over to a street light so I could see my watch. Twelve o'clock. It was Christmas, a time to be with loved ones. A few hours before I had been on the top of the world, at that moment I never had felt so alone. I was still too angry to go home so I headed out of town in the opposite direction.

"Back in those days there wasn't much on that side of town. The houses thinned out pretty fast. There were fields on each side of the road. It was lonely, but it was just where I wanted to be. Walking in the cold, listening to the small sounds of snow crunching under foot and the wind in the trees kept my mind off my problems.

"Suddenly a truck came over a hill and around a curve. The driver never saw me. I saw the truck just in time to dive out of its way. I scrambled to my feet. As I brushed myself off I realized that walking along a dark, deserted road might get me killed. I still wasn't ready to head back. Then I saw it. The snow clouds had blown away leaving a crystal clear sky filled with stars. There was one star that caught my attention. It seemed a little brighter than the others. I didn't remember seeing it there before. Stretched out between it and me was a field covered by snow. It was virgin, not a footprint in sight. I couldn't resist. I headed for the star.

"I do not know if I can adequately describe the experience of walking across that field. There was the crunch, crunch, crunch of fresh snow under foot and the soft sounds of blowing snow. There was more though. It was like I was exploring a new world for the first time. It was exhilarating. It was so exhilarating that when I finally came to the other side of the field I did something stupid. I should have turned back. There was a band of trees between me and what looked like another field. It was dark. The ground was littered with obstacles. But I was the intrepid explorer. No obstacle was too great for me.

"I headed into the trees. I got about half the way to the next field when my way was blocked. I went one way and then another trying to get around. I decided to go back. I couldn't see my star. My sense of direction was gone. Distracted, I tripped, fell, and hit my head. In that fraction of time before I lost consciousness I thought, 'I'm going to die.'

"The next thing I knew I was in the middle of a street with people yelling at me. They were all calling me terrible things in some strange language that I understood perfectly. I was turning this way and that, trying to get out of the way, but I kept bumping into people and making it worse. Finally, a squad of soldiers came past. The leader picked me up and threw me against a wall. I scrambled to my feet and found a space between two buildings in which to hide.

"For the next hour or so I watched this street scene shaking in fear. Hundreds of people flowed past. Most were on foot and carried their belongings. A few had donkeys or carts in which to transport their goods. All were dressed in some robe-like affair with sandals on their feet. I found I was wearing the same. Some appeared to walk alone, but the vast majority traveled in family groups with men, women, and children. The street was just dirt. The dust was awful. I couldn't see many buildings from my hiding spot, but they all seemed to be one story and made of some kind of stone. A few had awnings toward the street with merchants hawking their wares. It was all so bewildering to me. I knew I must be in hell. I just waited for the devil to come and laugh in my face.

"Night fell and the tide had turned into a trickle. I was just thinking I might leave my hiding spot to explore when I felt a sharp jab in the ribs. 'Your life or your purse.'

"My hands instinctively reached for the sky. Before I could say anything I was jabbed in the ribs a little deeper. 'I said, "Your life or your purse."'

"I didn't know what to say. I didn't know if I had a purse. Before I could think of anything to say my attacker shoved me against the wall, but at least the knife was no longer in my ribs. 'What is wrong with you? Can you not talk? Just hold still while I search you.'

"An expert hand went over me. When the search was finished I was spun around and found a knife aimed at my throat. 'Have you no rings, no necklace?' I showed him my hands and opened my robe.

"The knife fell away and my attacker laughed. 'You are even poorer than me. Your clothes are not worth stealing. You must be a beggar. I thought all you beggars stayed near the temple. I could use you though. I could use another man to help carry people into the alleyways after I bash them in the head. I do not like searching them out in the open and some of these merchants are too fat for me to drag away. How about it? Want to earn a little honest money?'

"I stood there in silence. After a few seconds had passed he said, 'No, is it? You beggars are all alike. Never want to work for anything. Just want it handed to them.'

"He turned to walk away. I let him take a few steps before I blurted out, 'Friend, what town is this?'

"He turned around and said, 'You really are lost.'

"'Yes, I am. I have no idea where I am or what I am doing here.'

"'This town is Bethlehem and all those people you saw are here being counted by the stinking Romans. The only good thing about all this is there are a lot more fat cats to steal from. I have to be off. No sense in wasting the dark.'

"Then he was gone. What he had told me left me more bewildered than before. Bethlehem, the city of David, and a Roman census, it was all so strange. A few minutes passed before it all sunk in. Warily I inched out to the street where a few stragglers, their way lit by the moon, slouched toward Bethlehem. I looked down the roadway in the direction of their passing. All I had to do was follow after them and who knew what a little searching around might turn up. I ran up the alley way instead.

"I ran through gardens and past livestock. Chickens squawked and dogs barked. People yelled. Still, I ran and I ran until I thought I was free. When I had cleared the detritus of civilization I stopped to catch my breath. And then I heard it, a baby's cry on the still night air. Turning toward the sound I saw a light. Without thinking I found myself moving toward the light. Then there it was. The light was coming from a cave. The front of the cave had one of those wooden awnings set over it. There was a fence enclosing an area where some animals appeared bedded down for the night. I realized then that I hadn't been running away from something. I had been running to it. I walked over to the fence, climbed over, and approached the hut.

"Joseph came out wielding a staff. 'Please, sir, do not come here. We have nothing for you and my wife has a new born babe,' he said as he approached me.

"I went right up to him, held out my hand, and said, 'You must be Joseph.' He was a little bewildered at hearing a stranger use his name so he let his staff drop to his side and took my hand uncertainly. By the moonlight I looked him over. He had a full beard, but he was younger than me.

"I let his hand drop and turned toward his wife. 'This must be Mary,' I said as I approached her. Then I fell on my knees at her side and said, 'And this must be Jesus.'

"Joseph was making some confused sounds behind me at hearing me use all their names, but I was concentrating on the mother and child. Mary was so beautiful. Her hair was covered, but her eyes and smile were something special. Even in the moonlight her skin glowed. She was so young, just a teenager really. The infant Jesus appeared to me to be unremarkable, just a perfect example of every other healthy newborn that has gone before or since.

"A thought came to me. I said to Mary, 'May I hold him?' I turned to Joseph and then back to Mary and said, 'Please, may I hold him. I am a father. I have held newborns. It would mean so much to me. Please.'

"Joseph wouldn't have let me, but Mary handed him over. How can I describe the feeling of holding the infant Jesus in my arms. Words are not adequate. There is a special feeling at holding your own children for the first time. This was like holding every newborn baby in your arms at the same time and have them all be yours. I have never known such a feeling of joy. I have never been happier, yet the tears rolled down my cheeks.

"A flash of lightening and a peal of thunder broke my reverie. From the pinnacle I plunged to the depth of despair. It was wrong. What right had I to hold the infant Jesus? I didn't belong there.

"I handed Jesus back to Mary and headed away from the hut. Joseph ran after me saying, 'Wait! Stranger, wait! Who are you? Do not leave us.'

"He caught up to me as I climbed over the fencing. I turned back to him and offered my hand. He took it. Not knowing what else to say I told him, 'Take care.'

"'Please,' he said, 'who are you that knows all our names? Why should you, a stranger, love my child this way? I did not mean to give offense. Stay with us as a friend.'

"'I do not belong here,' I told him. 'I must go.'

"I ran toward the thunder. I don't know what fueled me that night, but I ran like the wind. On and on I ran up into the hills. Lightning flashed, thunder roared, winds blew, and, finally, rains poured down. I kept going until I just stopped.

"In the dark of night a lightning flash revealed three boys of thirteen or fourteen hiding behind a rock. I went over to them. Before I could say anything one of them said, 'Please, sir, do not kill us.'

"One of the others said, 'Take all that we have, sir, but spare us, I beg of you.'

"'What's wrong with you boys?' I asked. 'What makes you think that I have come to harm you?'

"Lightning struck near-by and the three boys shivered with fear. 'It is the storm, sir. It is the worst that any of us have known. We thought it was sent by God to punish us. Then you appear out of nowhere and show no fear. You must be the messenger of God come to punish us.'

"The thought that I could be a messenger from God was so bizarre I wanted to laugh. I didn't want to frighten them so instead I smiled and said, 'No, I have not come to punish you. Why are you boys out here on a night like this?'

"'We have been tending our master's flock. The storm was so bad that the flock has scattered and we hid here rather than chase after them. In truth, sir, perhaps it would be better if you did punish us because our master will punish us cruelly in the morning if we lose even one lamb.'

"'It seems like you boys worry too much about being punished. Is life so bad for you?' I asked.

"'We are poor boys, sir. Someone is always beating us or calling us names. The only peace we have is on a quiet night out here with our flock and then we live in fear of robbers.'

"The rain had stopped. A wind had come up and with it an idea. I had to yell in order to be heard over the wind. 'Fear not, for, behold, I bring you tidings of great joy, which shall be to all people. For unto you is born this day in the city of David a Savior, which is Christ the Lord. And this shall be a sign unto you; you shall find the babe wrapped in swaddling clothes, lying in a manger.'

"When I had finished there was one more rumble of thunder in the distance. The wind died down and the dark became light. I turned and looked up. The clouds had parted revealing the brilliance of the moon.

"I turned to find the boys prostrating themselves in front of me. One of them said, 'You are the messenger of God and you have saved us from the storm. How may we serve you?'

"I lifted each of the boys to their feet saying, 'Not me. Do not worship me. Bethlehem is where you will find him. Go now and gaze upon him. The child's name is Jesus and his parents are Mary and Joseph. Go!'

"'The boys looked at each other. Without saying a word they appeared to come to a conclusion. 'We will seek this child and if it is as you say we will share the news that a savior is born with our friends.' Then they left in the direction of Bethlehem and I gazed at the moon in wonder.

"Again I felt compelled to run. I had no idea where I was headed or why I had to run to get there. It was the most glorious feeling. My senses were alert. There was the bright moon, the smell of the wet earth, and the rumble of distant thunder. I raced through the night with a feeling of freedom and power I had never known before or since.

"Then I stopped. Not because I was tired, but because I had reached my destination. And so I waited. In time a caravan appeared in the distance headed for where I waited. When it was close the leader called out to me, 'What town is that ahead?'

"'It is Bethlehem, the city of David, and I have just come from there,' I called back.

"With that the leader called a halt. There was a flurry of activity all along the caravan. Three men slipped their mounts and came over to me. They seemed to be arguing until they reached me. 'We three have come from our country following a star.'

"'A star?' I broke in.

"'Yes, that star.' one of them said and pointed in the direction of Bethlehem.

"I turned and there it was. Low on the horizon, it was a little brighter than the other stars, but mainly it was different. I had seen it before. It was the star that had led me out over that field of snow. Even then I found myself taking a few steps in its direction before I was called back by the sound of a voice, 'We have come because of a prophecy. There is to be a new king born who will rule the world in a different way. Have you heard of such a birth?'

"'I not only have heard of such a birth, but I have held the child.'

"They were quite excited now. 'Where can we find the child?'

"'You won't find the child in the town. Bethlehem is filled with travelers for a census. His parents, Mary and Joseph, were forced to seek shelter in a barnyard surrounded by beasts of the field. It was there, laying on a bed of straw, that I found Mary and the newborn Jesus. It was there, kneeling before her, that she gave me Jesus to hold and I experienced joy that is beyond words.'

"Their excitement increased. Two of them raced back to their mounts and the third waited behind to say, 'We must be off. With luck we can see this child before daylight. We are indebted to you. Won't you guide us to this source of your joy?'

"'No, I cannot. You will find the way, but I cannot show you.'

"With that, he ran back to his mount. As I watched the small caravan disappear in the direction of Bethlehem my heart was filled with hope. I was aimlessly backing away when I tripped and fell hitting my head.

"The next thing I knew some animal was licking my face. I had a sense of being frozen. A voice said 'Good Girl.' Two hands grabbed me hauling me to my feet. The world instantly spun. I was headed back down when an arm went around me. I felt lighter than air.

"I have some vague recollection of traveling over fields and through woods. A house appeared and we crossed the threshold into warmth. My wet clothes disappeared to be replaced by blankets. A fire roared as I sat in front of it. A cup of coffee appeared in my hand. I drank it greedily feeling its heat all the way down my throat into my stomach.

"A second cup replaced the first. I sipped at this and glanced at my rescuer. He was a big man with white hair and a full, white beard. He sat there puffing on a pipe gently stroking his dog. In my haze I could not help thinking that this was Santa Clause and, therefore, it had all been a dream. Perhaps it was summer and I had fallen asleep at my desk. Or maybe I would roll over and bump into my wife. Then the dream would end and the pain I had caused my wife would never have occurred.

"'How do you feel?' he asked.

"'Better, thank you,' I answered

"'That was quite a blow to the head. It doesn't look like you need any stitches and our skulls are pretty thick up there so I doubt you fractured it. Still, you probably ought to see a doctor when you get a chance. You'll have a headache for a few days.'

"My hand went to my scalp. A little pressure brought a twinge of pain. I looked at my fingers and found a few particles of dried blood.

"We were quiet for awhile. He puffed on his pipe. I stared into the flames. At last he said, "You wouldn't mind me asking what you were doing in the middle of nowhere tonight?'

"I didn't know what to say. I certainly did not want to discuss my private life with someone I did not know. I made believe I had not heard him and huddled into the blankets.

"'You do know this is Christmas?' he asked after awhile.

"He was not going to give up and I was starting to feel angry. I was searching for something to say when he said, 'You do know what Christmas is?'

"That did it. I was angry now. I turned on him and said 'Yes, I know what Christmas is.'

"'Good! I just wanted to be sure that I didn't have to call in the boys with the straightjacket.'

"'It's nothing like that. Okay,' I said and sat back down.

"'What is it like?' he asked.

"I jumped up again and stood over him. 'Look, old man, I don't know who you think you are, but….'

"I never did finish. He sat there fiddling with his pipe. Without looking up at me he said, 'I'm the man who saved your life.'

"I sat down and held my face in my hands. 'Yes, of course, I'm sorry. I don't know why I'm getting angry. There's just been so much pressure on me. Things have been…I don't know.'

"'It seems to me,' he said, 'that a man who was found freezing at night in the middle of nowhere couldn't have all the answers. Yet, whatever it was that drove him out there it allowed him to participate in a miracle.'

"I looked at him wondering how he could know. Was it a dream? I didn't know. The memory of dreams tends to fade, but I could remember every drop of rain, every peal of thunder. I looked down at my arms. I could still feel the newborn Jesus in my arms. He sat there puffing away on his pipe. I had to ask, 'What miracle?'

"'Well, maybe it's not a real big miracle, but think of it. A dog wakes up in the middle of the night. She manages to wake me up and gets me to take her outside. She runs off into the woods and I decide to follow. She runs through wood and field to find you lying on the ground unconscious. If we don't find you for another few hours you are probably dead. At the best, parts of you fall off from frostbite. Not a real big miracle, but it will do,' he said.

"'Yes, it will do,' I answered.

"'So, do you now what Christmas is?' he asked.

"'Are we back to that?' I asked him.

"'I just thought a man wandering around the woods in the middle of the night might be looking for answers. Christmas is as good a place as any to find them,' he said.

"He was right. I had been looking for answers. What could it hurt? I decided to play along. I told him, 'At Christmas we celebrate the birth of Jesus Christ.'

"'But?' he said.

"'But what? Isn't that what Christmas is all about?' I asked him.

"He sat there puffing on his pipe. He was not even looking at me. 'That is right as far as it goes,' he said. 'It just seems to me that if you were really celebrating the birth of Jesus you could not have been out there in the woods unconscious. There has to be a 'but.''

"He was right again. 'It has all become so commercial now. It's not just Christmas. It's everything. But with Christmas it has become worse. Christmas has become about advertising and presents and profits. The birth of Jesus seems to get lost in there somewhere,' I said.

"'It is a common refrain nowadays,' he said. 'The hurly burly of life just takes over. We lose the ability to relate to the most important events in our lives. What you need is something to help you take the sense of Christmas into your life.'

"'I don't understand,' I said.

"'The birth of Jesus is the birth of spirit in the form of matter,' he said.

"'Wait a minute. Spirit, matter, it is starting to sound like mumbo jumbo to me,' I said.

"'No,' he said, 'it is really quite simple. Have you ever held a newborn baby?' I looked at him. Did he know? He was not even looking at me. He held his arms cradling an imaginary baby. Without looking up he went on, 'When you hold a new born babe there is a sense of awe before the process of nature. When the child is your own there is a sense of gratitude for your participation in this miraculous process. The tiny child, so weak yet so full of potential, calls out of us a spontaneous love and compassion. And, finally, there is joy. Awe, gratitude, love, compassion, and joy, these are the emotions that the birth of Jesus is meant to give birth in your heart. Now comes the hard part. The birth of this spirit in your heart is like the birth of a newborn babe. It must be loved and cared for and nourished or it will die. So, hold the baby Jesus in your heart and every day is Christmas.'

"Now I was cradling an imaginary child. The weight I had felt in a dream had become real for me. The joy I had felt in a dream was real. And the tears of joy rolled down my cheeks.

"'Your clothes are dry. We ought to get you home,' he said.

"In silence I dressed. He ushered me out to his car. He had an old woody station wagon. His dog jumped into the passenger side, but when I opened the door she jumped into the back seat. The back was piled high with gaily wrapped presents. He caught me staring at all the presents and said, 'I make a few deliveries on Christmas morning.'

"He started off without asking for my address. I was too dazed to think of telling him. It was still dark out. After a couple of miles he asked, "What are you going to do?'

"'About what?' I responded.

"'I'm guessing here,' he said, 'but I took a look in your wallet. You have a nice family. One of the pictures was dated just a few weeks ago. I'm guessing you had a fight with your wife and went for a walk to figure it out. So, what are you going to do?'

"'I still haven't figured it out,' I said. 'Anything I can think of sounds like a poor excuse.'

"'That is a start.' he said. "Do not ruin a good apology with a poor excuse. In fact do not even use words. Show her your love. Remember, the word 'love' is just a four letter word compared to the real emotion. Show her how you feel and you will be alright.

"He came to a stop in front of our house. 'Here we are, John.' he said. 'Alice and Maggie are four and five, aren't they. I think I have some things here which will be just right for them.' He leaned over and rummaged around the back. Finally, he came up with two presents. He handed them over to me. I said, 'Thank you.' We shook hands and I got out of the car. His dog jumped into the front seat before I even closed the door.

I had crossed over to his side of the car when he rolled down his window and said, 'Merry Christmas, John.' Then he drove off.

It was like a light had been turned on. I ran after him, waving my free hand wildly, and yelled at the top of my lungs, 'Merry Christmas!' His arm came out the window and waved back. Then he turned a corner and was gone. I stood there in the middle of the road repeating 'Merry Christmas' over and over, watching where he had gone.

"Suddenly, I was seized by a new fire. I ran into the house, turned on the lights in the living room, and attacked the bare Christmas tree. I strung the lights. I hung the ornaments. A job that should have taken me four hours was over in less than one.

"I plugged in the lights. Stepping back to take a look at my handiwork I bumped into a table. I turned around. There she was, your mother, dear Jan. I do not know how long she had been watching. We looked at each other. She started to say something, but I reached her before it came out. I kissed her. I kissed her. I kissed her. And we both cried with joy.

"Alice and Maggie were up now. There were cries of 'Mommy' and 'Daddy.' Alice took one look at the tree and said, 'This is the best Christmas ever.'

"'Yes, Alice, I think you are right,' I told her.

My father stopped now. It had taken quite a bit of time to tell his story. Several times his voice had broken with emotion as he remembered that night. Now, in the silence, a thought occurred to me. "I was born nine months later."

"And you were born nine months later. Your mother and I had been trying to have another child for over two years. Nine months later I held you in my arms, but it was the memory of a dream, a dream when I was close to death, a dream of holding an infant born two thousand years ago that made every day Christmas for me. Now it is your turn. Perhaps your life is in the balance, not life or death, but how you will live. Remembering what Christmas is about and taking it to heart is as good as anyway to start. You have a long trip home. You'll have plenty of time to think."

I had fallen asleep in my clothes. All I had to do was find my shoes. As I left my hand found my father's shoulder in the dark. I gave it a squeeze and he gave my hand a pat.

As I left him sitting in the dark I said, "Merry Christmas, Dad."

"Merry Christmas, Son."

My father was wrong. It was not a long trip home.

Santa

It was Christmas Eve and life was good. I was at my son's house sitting in the dark, watching the lights twinkle on the Christmas tree, sipping a glass of eggnog when I heard my Grandson's voice, "Grandad?"

"Yes, Jason."

"Why do you always dress up like Santa Claus on Christmas?"

I looked over the costume I was wearing. It was still a bright red after all these years, fringed in white with black belt and boots. And the white beard was mine now. "Oh, I don't know why? It's just a habit I got into years ago. It's become sort of a tradition, I guess," I told him.

"That's not what Dad said."

I sat up and put down my drink. "What exactly does your Father say," I asked him.

"Well, I asked Dad why you always dressed up as Santa Claus on Christmas Eve. I thought you did it for me and my sister when we were little, but neither of us have believed in Santa for years so what's the point."

Jason stopped at this point, but I could see where he was going. "I'm sorry Jason. I guess it can be embarrassing to have a grandfather dressing up like this, but I wore this costume for years before you or Carol were born and I hope to wear it for years to come. I wear it, well, let's just say I wear it for a reason."

"That's what Dad said. He said there was a special reason you dressed up as Santa and there was a story to go with it. Dad said that if I wanted to hear the story I should ask you and say 'please.' So, please, Grandad, will you tell me the story?"

I looked out toward the kitchen where I knew my son was helping my daughter-in-law with dinner. I could hear their voices, but they were out of sight. I had told this story only once before. Over thirty years ago I had shared this with my son and he had remembered all these years. Then he had been part of the story. I didn't have to fill in a lot of blanks then. Now, where would I begin? How much should I tell? There were things I was not proud of.

"How old are you, Jason?"

"I'll be thirteen next month."

"That's about the age your Father was when this happened. I guess if he could live through it you can stand hearing the unvarnished truth. Sit down here and I'll see if I can get through the story before dinner.

"This all happened over thirty years ago. It was the first year your grandmother and I were divorced."

Jason interrupted, "But you and Grandma aren't divorced now."

"Hold your horses. You're jumping the story. We did get back together and this story led to it, but if you keep interrupting dinner will get cold. Now where was I?

"Your Grandmother and I were divorced. It was the right thing for her to do. I wasn't a very happy person. I drank too much and I flirted too much and when none of it made me any happier I blamed her. The worst part of it was being separated from your Dad. He was such a good kid. Before we were divorced he was always there so I could ignore him. After the divorce there was just a hole in my life. I couldn't believe anything could hurt so much.

"Then, right after the divorce I lost my job. The company I worked for was bought out the year before. At first everyone held their breath expecting our division to close right away. As time passed and our division turned a profit everyone breathed a sigh of relief expecting our jobs were safe. Then the axe fell on everybody. Still, I thought with my talents finding another job would be easy. The weeks became months and the months stretched on. I couldn't find a job. There were jobs I was perfect for, but they always took someone else.

"I had been paying alimony and child support right along. All my savings were gone and I wasn't sure how I was going to pay rent. I called up your Grandma to tell her I didn't have a job and couldn't make the next payment. 'No problem,' she said. She had found a job. The payments could wait. Instead of being happy for her it just made me angry.

"It was the week before Thanksgiving and I was getting desperate. No one was hiring for Christmas, yet. The want ads were pretty spare for anything I felt comfortable doing. Then I saw it. There was an ad for a Santa Claus, wanted right away, better than minimum wage, and guaranteed overtime.

"I called the number in the ad. It was a garden store that every year put on a big display of Christmas decorations complete with a Santa. Every year they sold a lot of Christmas trees, a lot of decorations, and a lot of lights. The job hadn't been filled. I would be right over.

"I drove across town as fast as I could. When I arrived at Racker's I was directed to the office. I walked into the office and told the secretary I was there to interview for the Santa job. Edith had been with Mr. Racker forever. She took one look at me and said that I wasn't what they were looking for. I wouldn't leave it alone. I begged. I pleaded. I did everything but cry on cue. Finally, Edith said she would ask Mr. Racker. She went into the inner office, came out a few minutes later, and motioned me through the door.

"Mr. Racker was something of an institution. My parents had taken me to Racker's when I was a kid. Back then Mr.Racker had played Santa some of the time so it was quite likely I had sat on his knee and asked for a new sled or a baseball bat. I took your Dad there a couple of times and every year the Christmas display was bigger and better.

"I did not know what to expect when I stepped into the office and suddenly I was so nervous I couldn't say a word. Mr. Racker looked me up and down and said, 'What makes you think you can play Santa Claus?'

"The words came flying out of my mouth. I told him of my experience as an actor. How that experience would help me play Santa. How I had experience with make-up and would guarantee that I would look the part. Then I told him how badly I needed the job. I didn't plan on saying anything about that. It just came out. Finally, I told him I just wanted a shot. I asked for two days. If I wasn't the best Santa they ever had he could fire me and I would still thank him for giving me a chance.

"Then there was quiet. He looked up at me and I looked down at him. I could see that I hadn't convinced him. I hadn't said the right thing. It was another failure. I could feel myself crumbling inside when Mr.Racker reached out and flipped the intercom. 'Edith,' he said, 'we're going to give this young man a chance. Give him our Santa Claus suit and have him report to you tomorrow at 9 am.'

"Mr. Racker stood up and held out his hand. As I shook hands with him he said, 'Good luck, Son.'

"I thanked him profusely and guaranteed him he would not be sorry. Edith was waiting with the Santa Claus suit when I left the office. She told me to report to her at the office the next day wearing the Santa Claus suit. I was to start the next day.

"I don't know why I wanted that job so bad. I was desperate and the overtime pay was appealing, but Santa Claus? Whatever reason, I was as high as a kite as I drove back to my apartment. I tried the suit on right away. I tried a variety of padding until I found a combination that worked.

Next I turned to the makeup. In the yellow pages I found a store that had theatrical makeup. I drove over and picked out the items I needed. When I got back to my apartment I tried it all out. Checking myself in the mirror I saw the perfect Santa.

"I started to work on the delivery. I practiced laughs. I practiced getting the right pitch for my voice. I practiced over and over until it was natural. Then I started on scripts. I tried to think of every question and every child so I could cover all the bases. I practiced my delivery and when I would laugh and how I would laugh. I just kept going until early in the morning. I forgot to eat. I couldn't sleep. I kept on visualizing myself as Santa over and over and over.

"My alarm woke me. I couldn't have gotten more than two or three hours of sleep. After a couple of cups of coffee I got back into costume and was waiting for Edith when she arrived for work. She gave me the once over and said, 'Not bad.' Edith gave me some forms to sign then led me to the Christmas Kingdom. All the way she kept up a monologue on dos and don'ts for Santas. When she left me at Santa's throne she said, 'You look a lot better than last year's Santa. Good luck.'

"I was alone then. When it was busy there would be someone to help, but that day there wasn't going to be a crowd. There was a door on one side for families to enter, another through which they were to leave. The room was a spectacular display of Christmas lights. After taking it all in I sat and waited. The longer I sat the more convinced I was that I was in over my head. There was no way I could make all those little kids and their parents happy.

"A four year old and her mother were the first. It went pretty well. I felt a little better. A steady trickle of children showed up, just enough that I could spend a little time with them. By the end of the day I was feeling good about playing Santa. Off and on during the day I had seen Mr. Racker or Edith peaking through the doorway to check up on me.

"The next day went the same way. On Thanksgiving the store was closed. The day after Thanksgiving the store opened early. No one had mentioned anything so I showed up for the early opening. We were packed. It went on all day long. At noon my assistant started to close up for lunch, but there was a long line of kids waiting. I decided to skip lunch and continue to see the kids. I never saw Mr. Racker or Edith check up on me after that. A glass of milk and a plate of cookies showed up a little later.

"The next few weeks passed in a blur. I was just so happy to be working and picking up a paycheck. The day before Christmas Edith came by at the beginning of the day. She handed me an envelope, told me to report Mr. Racker's office at the end of the day, and wished me a merry Christmas. The envelope was a check for work through the end of the day. At lunch I rushed to the bank, cashed the check, and paid the rest of my back rent. I had enough cash left for a few weeks of groceries and a good Christmas present for your Dad.

"Racker's stayed open into the evening on Christmas Eve. I don't think Mr. Racker expected much business as there was only a skeleton crew at work. He just wanted people to have a place to go if they needed any last minute item for the perfect Christmas. I helped close up. I lingered and said some good-byes. I didn't relish going back to the ranks of the unemployed. Just as I was about to leave I remembered Edith asking me to see Mr. Racker in his office. I ran back in hoping he hadn't given up on me.

"I knocked on his door and heard, 'Come in.'

"I entered and said, 'I'm sorry if I've kept you waiting, Mr. Racker.'

"'Charley,' he said, 'I wanted to apologize to you.'

"I didn't think he knew my name. Now, he wants to apologize to me. I didn't know what to think or say so I just stood there.

"'I want to apologize because I did not think you would be a good Santa. When I asked you why you wanted to be Santa all you did was talk about yourself. I thought you were another one of those selfish types there are so many of today. You did not talk about Christmas or the children. I just gave you a chance because you so obviously needed one and it was the Christmas season. I think of myself as a generous man, but I fully expected to fire you in a couple of days. Instead you were good at the start and great at the end. You have no idea how many parents came in to tell Edith how wonderful you were.

"He paused. I still had no idea what to say or do. The few seconds passed and Mr. Racker said, 'I just wanted to let you know that I thought you were the best Santa I have ever seen and I wanted to give you this.'

"Mr. Racker held out an envelope. I took it. He indicated I should open it. I did and looked inside. There was $200 in there.

"'Merry Christmas, Charley. You deserve it,' Mr. Racker said.

"I told him, 'Thank you, thank you, thank you. You have no idea what this means to me.'

"I think I do,' he said. 'It is the best job in the world, Charley. You have a few minutes with each child to make them happy. Their parents cannot wait for that to happen. For just a moment you bring joy into their lives. That is what being Santa is all about.'

"Mr. Racker looked down at his watch. 'I did not realize it was getting so late,' he said. 'Time for both of us to be headed home.'

"I turned to go. Then I remembered the Santa suit. 'I don't have a change of clothes. I'll have to return the Santa suit after Christmas, Mr. Racker.'

"'Do not worry about it, Charley. Keep it as a gift. Just remember to put it to good use,' he said.

"We walked out to the parking lot in silence. Ours were the last two cars there. We waived each other a merry Christmas and I thanked him again. I got in my car and watched him drive off.

"I was feeling pretty good about the world when I turned the key and nothing happened. I tried again and again. There were no lights. The radio didn't work. I opened the hood. Everything appeared to be connected. The battery was dead. I couldn't call anybody to give me a jump at that hour on Christmas Eve. It wasn't too cold. The night was clear. I decided to walk home. It wouldn't be much more than an hour.

"I was still feeling good about life as I headed for home. The path I took went through a rather bleak section of town. To go around it would have added almost another hour to my walk. I didn't think much about it until I started hearing noises. I tried to glance over my shoulder without looking too conspicuous. There appeared to be three of them. I walked a little faster and turned a corner. They still followed. I turned another corner. They were right behind me. Then I ran. What a sight that must have been, a running Santa? I ducked down an alley way hoping to lose them, but they were right behind. Someone tackled me. I was hit in the back of the head. Things went dark.

"Someone was poking me. I heard a voice say, 'Are you all right, mister.'

"Slowly, I pulled myself back to consciousness. I opened my eyes and recoiled in fright. A face leaned over me and as I backed against a wall trying to get away he said, 'Why are you so afraid? Is it because my face is black?'

"I didn't say anything. I couldn't say anything. Then he stepped back where there was a little more light and said, 'Do not be afraid. We have more in common than you know. Besides, would Santa Claus hurt you?'

"I looked him over in the dim light. He was wearing a Santa Claus costume. Somehow I wasn't afraid anymore. I think I even smiled. He reached down and offered me a hand up. I took it, but when I was upright I almost passed out again. He put his arm around me and we headed for his home. He was a jolly old fellow. He talked a steady stream as he guided me along. I don't remember much of what he said except for the part about cutting through that alleyway on his way home.

"We reached his home and he deposited me on a couch. He disappeared. When he returned he poured something on my scalp that burned like the dickens. He pulled over a light to examine my head. 'I do not think you need any stitches,' he said, 'but you ought to go to the hospital.'

"The thought of doctor's bills flashed through my head. 'No doctors,' I told him.

"'Okay,' he said, 'how about a cup of coffee?'

"When he had left to make the coffee I remembered my wallet. I searched. It was gone and so was the envelope that Mr. Racker had given me. I was broke again. I was cursing my luck when he set a cup of coffee in front of me. 'What is wrong?' he asked.

"I told him about being robbed of all my money. He made some comment about being broke was especially hard at Christmas time. I told him it was even worse. It was the first Christmas since my divorce and I really wanted to get my son a special present. Now, I wouldn't be able to get him anything. I felt like such a failure.

"'Let me tell you a story,' he said. 'This happened a long time ago down south where I grew up. I was a young man still living at home with my parents. We had a small farm that I helped my Daddy work. I did some odd jobs in town to make a little extra money. We did not have a lot, but what we had we enjoyed. Momma, well, my Momma could cook and I did like to eat, especially her sweet potato pie.

"'I had heard about Santa Claus. One year I got it in my head that it would be nice to play Santa for some of the children. I bought some cloth. My Momma helped me make a Santa Claus suit. She baked up a special batch of cookies. The last couple of days before Christmas I put on the Santa suit, visited all our friends with little children, and gave out the cookies.

"'Those little children did not have much so getting a visit from Santa and a cookie lit them right up. The smiles, the laughter, the hugs, and the kisses, there could not have been anything better. I was hooked.

"'I spent the next year fixing up the Santa suit and scrounging to make each of those children a toy. Some of our friends who lived further away had heard about my playing Santa and talked to Momma. So, my list grew. That was all right. It was not more work. It was more joy.

"'I started my rounds almost a week before Christmas. The nights were chilly and the walks were long. I was so high after playing Santa for those poor little children that I never gave it no mind.

"'It was Christmas Eve and I was headed home after my last stop. A car pulled up on the side of the road. I never gave it a thought. I did not know anyone who owned a car. Then someone called out something that froze my heart. I turned to see four men dressed in sheets running toward me. I took off. Unfortunately, I am not built for speed. They caught up to me and knocked me down. I curled up into a ball and covered my head. They kicked me and beat me, called me "Fatty" and "Boy" and several other names I do not want to mention, and the last thing I heard before passing out was "Serves you right for trying to be Santa."

"'Someone was poking at me. At first I decided to play possum, but he continued to poke at. Then I heard him say, "Are you all right? I have come to help you."

"'I opened my eyes to find a pale face wearing a pale robe. I pulled away thinking it was one of those men who had beaten me. The man smiled and said, "Do not be afraid. I have come to help you."

"'He turned and called to his camp. Several men came and carried me to the camp. I was brought to a tent where I was bathed and dressed and fed. Everyone treated me royally. It was so strange for a poor, country boy like me to be waited on. While I was eating three men came in and sat down. One of them was the man who came to my aid. He introduced each of them and then asked my name. I was going to say "Sammy," but I caught myself and said, "Samuel."

"'This brought about much excited discussion among the three of them. They seemed to think the name Samuel was a wonderful thing. Then their leader asked if I had a family name. I could not tell them "Jefferson" so I said, "I come from a long way from here so my family name would not be familiar to you, but my Father's name was Solomon."

"'Again, there was much excited discussion among the three. The leader was beaming when he finally turned back to me. "It is decided," he said. "You must accompany us. It is propitious."

"'Things were strange enough without suggesting I should come along with them. I was quite grateful for there help, but I was thinking it was time to sneak out the back door and find my way home to Momma. For some reason I felt compelled to ask, "Where is it you are headed?"

"'The leader looked puzzled. "As a traveler we thought you knew. We have come following a star. This star is a portent of the birth of a new king that shall rule the world in a new way. Surely, you have come following the same star."

"'I was just confused. Without thinking I said, "Star! What star?"

"'The leader stood up and took my arm. "Come, Samuel," he said. "Come out into the night and I will show you."

"'We went outside and walked away from the camp. He pointed up and said, "See, Samuel, the star."

"'There it was. The sky was not like what we see today. It was ablaze with stars. But this one, well, I felt myself drawn to it. I walked toward it as if a few more steps would take me closer to a star millions of miles away. Behind me my guide told me that they had come from their land far to the east following the star all the way. They had been to see the King of the Hebrews, but he had not been helpful. Now they were making their way to Bethlehem where they hoped to find the newborn king.

"'Three travelers in search of a newborn king, a wondrous star, Bethlehem, I knew where I was now. Without taking my eyes from the star I said, "He will lead a humble life, yet his life will be a light unto the ages."

"'My guide was very excited by this remark. "You know, Samuel. You know," he said. "You must come with us now. We must retire now so that we can start early. Come. Come with me and I will show you to your tent."

"'My guide walked me back and showed me a tent in which to sleep. Someone would come for me in the morning. I lay there, but could not sleep. How had I gotten there? Was I dead? Thoughts passed through my brain, but now that I had seen the star nothing else mattered. The star called to me and I went outside, to the edge of the camp. There I sat down and watched the star. I was going to Bethlehem.

"'They found me asleep under the stars. I was given some fruit for breakfast while the camp was packed up. Some camels were used for baggage, but I and my guide walked. He was quite excited at approaching Bethlehem. It had been a long and arduous trip. He and his friends had despaired of finding the child that they sought. Now, I was with them to show the way. I tried to explain that I did not know the way. He would have none of it. His questions made me search all those Bible lessons my

Momma used to give me. Momma could read and her son was going to read. The Bible was about all we had to read in those days.

"'The trip to Bethlehem had gone quickly. We arrived just after the sun had gone down. Now, they all turned to me. "Where will we find the child," they asked. I told them I did not know the way, but that he would be found in a stable or cave lying in a manger.

"'We searched the town asking after a newborn as we went. No one seemed to know anything. Then I heard it, a cry. It was so faint that I was not sure at first. The sound came again. I followed it and they followed me. I went out beyond the edge of town. There I saw a light. The light was coming from a wooden hut backed up against a hollow in the rock. A crude fence held in some barnyard animals. And there, at the center, was a mother holding a child.

"'As we approached, Joseph came out and told us that only himself, his wife, and their newborn were there. Please, would we leave them in peace? My guide took over as spokesman now. He explained that they were learned men who had come along way in search of his son. They had come to pay homage to him for it was written that his son would be a great king who would rule the world in a new way. They had offerings and if they would be permitted to gaze upon his son and make their offerings they would leave and peace be upon you.

"'Joseph relented and they sent for their pack animals. The offerings were brought out and the three crossed over the fence. My guide turned back to me and said, "Samuel, you are not coming?"

"'Rather sheepishly I told him that I had nothing to offer. "Ah, Samuel," he said, "I am surprised at you. The presents that we bring are gold, frankincense, and myrrh. What are these to a newborn child? The presents are tokens of our love. Love is the true gift we have to offer. You, Samuel, have brought love, the true gift."

"'He put his arm around my shoulders and together we approached Mary and her baby. The other two wise men had already presented their offerings and were kneeling before the manger. My guide set his present on the ground before him and kneeled down. I was still uncertain what to do. Then, Mary looked up at me and smiled. I smiled back and turned my gaze on Jesus. Perhaps his appearance was that of any other sleeping babe, but seeing him I was filled with such a sense of joy that I fell on my knees and pledged my love.

"'Then I woke up. I was looking up at a sky filled with stars. When I tried to move the pain brought back the memory of those awful men. Yet, I was happy. Those foolish men had meant to rob me of my joy. Instead, I had experienced joy beyond all measure.

"'I lay there by the side of the road unable to move, but strangely feeling no pain. The memory of Mary's smile and the infant Jesus was fresh in my mind. And when I looked up at the sky I thought I saw the star.

"'They found me early in the morning. My Father brought the wagon and carted me home. It took a couple of weeks for me to heal completely. When I had healed I started right in on my plans for playing Santa Claus for the next Christmas. There was no way I would let those men rob me of my joy. Oh, I traveled over fields and through woods instead of along roads, but I was going to play Santa.

"'Momma died a few years later. My Father died the next year. I decided to head north looking for work. Every year, though, I have played Santa as much as I can. I give the children a toy or some candy. The real gift I give is the few minutes of love I offer in memory of the one child. Love is the real gift, the only gift that anyone can offer.'

"Samuel was silent then. Our eyes met and he smiled. I looked around the room. There was a Christmas tree hung with all sorts of Santas. There was a sleigh, reindeer, and Santas here, there, and everywhere.

"My eyes came back to Samuel and his smile. I felt myself smiling back. And as we looked at each other our grins just got bigger and bigger. Then I realized that I had walked into that house worried about my head and my money and my misery and somehow Samuel had given me a new life.

"The moment was broken by the sound of a church bell. Samuel pulled out his watch. 'It is Christmas. I have to get to church. We have a midnight ceremony every year. If I do not get over there people will be wondering after my health. Are you feeling alright? You are welcome to come with me or if you do not feel up to walking yet you can stay here until I get back.'

"I stood up. 'I feel fine, no, I feel great,' I told him. 'I think I should be getting home, but I would like to walk with you to your church.'

"We left the house. I followed his lead and a few blocks later the sounds of Christmas carols hung about us as we approached a small church. Samuel offered his hand and I took it. After saying good-bye and wishing me a merry Christmas he made to go, but I wouldn't let go of his hand. 'Samuel,' I said, 'thank you.'

"'No, Charley, thank you,' he said, 'I see in you great things. Just keep in mind what the real gift is and you will never lose your way again.'

"I let him go and watched him walk up to the church. At the church door he turned, waved, and called, 'Merry Christmas to all and to all a goodnight.' Then he laughed. He disappeared into the sounds of carols and bright light. I did not think of it at the time, but I don't remember telling him my name.

"I floated home. Nothing on that walk left an impression on my memory until I reached my apartment house. Before I went inside I looked up at the sky. I don't know what I was expecting to see. There was only one star. One star was enough.

"I went up to my apartment. Suddenly I felt very sleepy. I barely managed to make it to the bedroom where I fell on the bed and went into a deep sleep.

"When I woke up it was sunny out. I checked the clock. It was a few minutes past noon. I lay there wondering if the events of the night before had been a dream. My hand went to my scalp and when I felt the pain I knew it must have been real. Also, I knew that I didn't have a minute to lose. I was still dressed as Santa, but I had to walk over to your Gandma's house before she left for her parent's and Christmas dinner. Our custody agreement gave her Christmas day. If I called she would just tell me not to come. She might even leave early. I got up and ran out the door. I had to see my son.

"Half an hour later I was ringing the doorbell. Your Grandma answered the door. She looked me up and down in my Santa suit, but didn't say a word about it. 'You aren't supposed to be here,' she said. 'You get Tommy tomorrow.'

"'I know,' I said. 'I'm sorry. Something's happened and I would really like to talk to Tommy for a little while. Please.'

"Your Grandma thought about it for awhile then stepped aside telling me, 'Tommy's in his room.'

"I went upstairs and found your Dad playing with his Christmas presents. He was excited to see me. After we hugged I asked him to sit down and told him the story I just told you. When I was finished I said to him, 'Tommy, I had to come over today to tell you that I might be broke, I might be out of a job, I might embarrass you, but I will always love you.'

So you see, Jason, that night I found my life. Every year I play Santa to honor Samuel who taught me that the real gift is the gift of love. Just as Samuel did I offer each child a few minutes of love in memory of the one child who's birth we celebrate.

"Well, that's the reason I dress up as Santa every year. And I'm going to continue dressing up as Santa until I can't anymore. Then I'm going to miss it. What do you think?"

Jason through his arms around me and said, "I love you, Grandad."

"I know, Jason. I love you, too."

Judas

I poked my head into the office and gave a little knock. When the occupant looked up I said, "Jack, you wanted to see me?"

"Kate, come on in and have a seat. We need to talk."

I crossed the room to the proffered chair. I had been in this office many times before, but I was always impressed. It was a corner office with full windows on two sides looking out over a park like campus The two walls were paneled in a dark mahogany to match the mahogany desk. The carpet was just the right side of dark amber to set off the mahogany. The carpet felt so soft under foot that I always wanted to take off my shoes.

Jack finally finished up and turned his attention to me. "I am sorry to pull you in here on the Friday before Easter, but there is a problem with your Singapore deal."

"I don't understand. The contracts are supposed to be signed in two weeks. How can there be a problem and I don't know about it?"

"Evidently, this one went CEO to CEO," he said. Holding up his hand to forestall my objections Jack continued, "It is not the way it is supposed to be, but especially in Asia that is the way it works sometimes. I think the CEO of the Singapore company was out on the golf course with another CEO. You know how it works. Their kids are at UCLA together. Then the CEO of our competitor hints that this may not be the best deal. So, the Singapore CEO wants to run the numbers again. It may be a pain, but it is not unreasonable."

I could not believe it. "It's the French, isn't it? There's no one in Asia who can do what we can do."

Jack shook his head. "I do not think it is the French this time. And you are right. There is no one in Asia that can do what we can do, but they may try to buy the expertise. In fact they may try to buy you."

Jack paused. I was too angry to bite on that last tidbit so Jack went on, "They want you in Singapore on Wednesday their time. Originally, they wanted you there on Monday, but Steve would not have it. He explained that it would be unfair to you to have to travel on the Easter weekend so they settled on Wednesday. You can leave Sunday afternoon and arrive early Tuesday so you will have a day to get over the jet lag. Is there a problem?"

Jack was good. I didn't think it showed. Yes, there was a problem. The kids were off from school next week and we had planned a trip. The Singapore deal was big, big for me, big for the corporation. I looked him square in the eyes. "No, there was no problem."

"Good! Then I can move on to the other thing I wanted to talk to you about. Jerry Wilson is retiring in a few months. I am slated to take his position. Right now you are the list that I will recommend to take over this division. I cannot promise anything, but closing this deal could make the difference."

I was stunned. Becoming the vice president of a division was the next major stepping stone, but I had not expected an opening for another year. "Thank you, Jack. I appreciate the confidence."

"You deserve it. You have always gone the extra mile for us and your work has been outstanding. I have made it clear to the board that you have talent and if they want to keep that talent they need to put it to work at the next level. If they decide to go in a different direction I expect you will have to consider your options. I know I would. Now, is there anything else I can do for you."

Jack both meant and did not mean that last remark. After working with him for eight years I knew it was his way of indicating that the meeting was over. I got up and told him, "No, you have really done quite enough."

Jack got up and escorted me to the door. We shook hands as I left and he told me, "Make us look good on this one," before wishing me a good weekend.

I decided not to do any more work that day other than gather all the information I would need for my presentation. That task was not very hard as 99% was on the computer. I had given the same presentation several times so the plane trip to Singapore would be plenty of time for review. Then I stopped by the travel office and booked the flights and hotel.

I left the office a little earlier than usual. The parking lot was still over half full when I left in my convertible. The day was beautiful so I put the top down. I loved driving that convertible. It was way too expensive and really only seated two, but I had to have it. It was red. It was hot. It was me. I even learned how to drive a standard shift. On the open road the convertible was awesome.

I could not believe it. I was going to be vice president of a division. I deserved it, but sometimes you do not believe it is going to happen until it does. I had put in a lot of extra time and effort to get where I was. First, there had been college. I hated school, but I was good at it so I had my pick of business schools. Then there was business school. I still hated school. I did well, but the only thing I really liked about business school was Eric. How lucky was I to meet him? He was a reporter. Somehow we met and it was the right thing from the first minute. We got married after business school. My first job was local so Eric could keep his job. Then I got pregnant with the twins, Alice and Allison. Eric gave up his job at the paper to write freelance and stay home with the girls. I spent the next two years working extra hard to make up for the time I missed giving birth. Then the headhunter called. It was a new job with a new company in a new city. It meant more money, a bigger house, and the promise of bigger things to come. I worked like a dog, but it was finally happening.

I floated home that day with every kind of thought running through my head. I couldn't remember anything about the trip home when I pulled into the driveway. I called out, "Eric," as I entered the house.

Eric's answering "Kate" came from upstairs. Seconds later he appeared carrying an overstuffed laundry basket.

"You're home earlier than I expected,' he said as he leaned over to kiss me. "Is Jack finally mellowing in his old age?"

Eric did not wait for an answer disappearing into the basement with the laundry. "As a matter of fact I had a talk with Jack today," I called down the stairs after him. "He told me that Jerry Wilson was retiring and he was going to take Jerry's place."

Eric reappeared at the top of the steps. "That's your job, then. I mean you've worked so hard for so long you deserve to take over from him. Don't tell me that old rascal's going to recommend someone else."

"No, he's going to recommend me."

Eric rushed over to give me a hug. "That's great," he said. "It is finally going to happen. For awhile there I thought we might have to make another move."

"There is a problem, though."

Eric backed off and gave me a look. "Why don't I like the sound of that?" he said.

"I have to be in Singapore this week."

Eric put some distance between us. I could see how much this upset him. "How could you do this? We've been planning this trip for six months. The kids are all excited about it and now you have to throw it all away."

"The Singapore deal is a really big deal. You know that. You know how much time I've put into it. It isn't my fault. Someone got to the CEO of the Singapore company suggesting they could do it for a better price. I have to go back and run the numbers for a little reassurance. I thought this deal was in the bag. Do you think I want to go back there?"

"This trip is a big deal, too. At least it is to me and the girls," Eric told me.

"Do you think I like disappointing the girls?" I asked him. "Listen. This is a sacrifice for me. This is what I need to do to succeed. And with the success we'll have plenty of money to put the girls in private school and send them to whatever college they want to go to. It's what we decided on."

I could see Eric was very upset, but when he spoke he tried to remain calm. "No! It is what we agreed to. There is a difference. And don't you bring up money. The girls and I could be happy on what I make. And don't you ever mention sacrifice. Let me tell you about sacrifice. Every week since the girls have been born and I gave up my job I would get calls offering me freelance jobs. If I can't do it by phone or internet I turn it down. But I am going to tell you that it is not a sacrifice because I am taking care of the two best kids on the face of this planet. I am doing what I love so the fact that my career is in the toilet doesn't matter. It is only a sacrifice if you're giving up something you love. Whereas you are in love with success and money and expensive toys so you are doing the thing you love."

"Eric, how can you be so cruel. I love you. I love the girls."

"Yes, you do, in your way. I should have known better. I always knew you had this passion for success. I always thought it was childish and you would grow out of it. You were so bright and beautiful. I chose to overlook it. I thought I saw something else in you, something that might grow with marriage and a family. Boy, was I wrong. You couldn't wait to get back to work after the kids were born. I think we are really just baubles on a chain you get to dangle around your neck to prove you can have it all."

I fought back tears as I told him, "This is so unfair. I've been a good mother and wife. You've never said anything like this before."

Eric charged across the room and grabbed me by the shoulders. His eyes were angry. He was shaking with emotion and he shook me. I had never seen him like this. He scared me. "You have no idea what it takes to be a good mother and wife," he said as he shook me. "You've defined being a good mother and wife as being what you do. You live in your own little reality where you think buying expensive presents makes up for not really loving someone. Well, let me tell you this. Your girls are on the verge of becoming young women. They need a mother and I need a wife."

Then it happened. I slapped him. I don't think I've ever heard a louder sound. It seemed to go on and on. Then we stood there staring at each other, gasping with emotion. Finally, Eric said, "I have to pick up the girls."

Without moving I watched the front door close behind him. I heard the van start and drive away. I was alone. I've never felt so alone and I never want to feel that alone again. The tears were coming now, but I had to decide what to do. I couldn't face Eric when he had the girls. I needed to get out of there. I needed to think.

I took off in my car, happy to be doing one thing I could enjoy. Then I hit the interstate. It was the beginning of a beautiful, holiday weekend. The traffic crawled along for hours. At last I broke free and let the motor out. But where was I headed?

Without thinking I was headed for my mother's house. I didn't know whether I really wanted to go there. She lived a full day's drive away and it was already dark out. Still, the interstate between here and there was usually wide open and fun to drive. So, without making any real decision, on I drove, zooming around slower cars and trucks with the CD turned up too loud. I would take it to the edge of where I felt safe thinking that danger would force me to concentrate and block out stray thoughts. It worked for a few minutes. Then I would hear the sound of that slap again, louder each time until it was a thunderclap.

I was doing eighty, uphill, passing a truck when an alarm went off. My heart skipped a couple of beats until I realized I was just running low on gas. I pulled off at the next exit. When I had filled up with gas it was like I had hit a wall. The adrenalin of the road had kept me awake. Now I felt tired. I went into the convenience store to grab a cup of coffee and some chocolate. On the way out the clerk looked at me. Normally, I would barely notice the clerk and she would barely notice me. This one seemed to really look at me as if she was judging me. I sat in the car eating my snacks, trying to shake off that feeling. Then I realized my makeup must be a mess from all my tears. I turned on a light to check my face, wiped off the smears, and felt a little better.

A couple of more hours went by on the road. In the end I was having trouble concentrating enough to keep up to the speed limit. I was trying to force the car up a steep hill when I drifted off the road. The spray of gravel brought back that adrenalin rush and I jerked the car to safety. I crawled up the rest of the hill and pulled off at a scenic overlook hoping some fresh air might wake me up.

I was alone again. The only sound was the distant whine of gears as the trucks shifted going up and down the hill. I yelled out, "It's not fair." There was no one to hear me. I wanted to cry and I wanted not to cry. Then I looked up. It was a clear night and there were stars everywhere. How long had it been since I looked up at the stars? My father had taken me out to look at the stars. He had me pick out a star. We looked it up in the library and we tracked it night after night. My father said that the star would always be there for me.

Now I searched the sky. I knew I couldn't recognize the same star after all these years, but perhaps I could find one that spoke to me. There was one, not the brightest in the sky, but it was what I was looking for. I sat there on the hood of my car looking at my star and I did not feel so alone.

The night was getting cold. The chill forced me back into the car where I headed down the interstate. In the valley I exited and headed toward the little town. It was not far before I saw a sign for a lodge that said it had a vacancy. I pulled off, got out, and rang the bell at the office. It had gotten really cold since I left the mountaintop and I was getting impatient when the door opened.

A head poked out and said, "What do you want?"

"Your sign said you had a vacancy. I need a room."

The man opened the door a little wider and stepped outside where he could look at the sign. "Well, how about that," he said, "I guess

I did forget to turn off the sign. We don't have any rooms. Full up. Sorry about that."

He headed back inside. Normally I would have blasted him, but I was too tired. "Please, sir, it's freezing out here. Couldn't I come in for just a few minutes?"

He looked me over. Then he looked at my car, then me again. "I guess I wouldn't feel right just letting you go at this hour. Come on in." He went inside and I followed.

When we were inside I asked him, "Isn't there some place I could stay the night?"

"Well, you could try the motel on the other side of the interstate, but I'm pretty sure they're full up, too."

"Is there any other town nearby?" I asked.

"The nearest town is about twenty minutes down the road."

I sat down heavily on a little bench discouraged at the news. "Twenty minutes! I almost had an accident on the interstate. I don't think I can drive another twenty minutes."

"They're probably full up, too, so I wouldn't worry about getting there anyway."

I sat there on the bench getting wearier by the second. We were both silent. Even though I had woken him up he was kind enough not to rush me out of there.

After a couple of minutes I asked, "Why are you so sure that all these places are going to be full up?"

"It happens this way every year at this time."

"How come?"

"Well, the church across the street is, well, I don't know how to put it so I guess I'll just say it's something special. Every year at this time the choirs from all the churches in this neck of the woods get together, over a hundred strong, and put on a concert on Easter morning. It's, well, it's quite a show. It's become quite a tradition in this neck of the woods so people and relatives come from all around to this little town to see it. Got to be so popular they had to put on extra services just so everyone could see. And afterward they have an Easter egg hunt and people have special parties."

"Sounds pretty nice," I told him.

"Makes people feel pretty good."

It did sound nice and it was all very interesting, but I was still without any place to sleep. Then it struck me, "Couldn't I sleep right here on this bench?"

"Nope. Can't let it happen."

"I'd be willing to pay."

"Sorry. If it was up to me I might let you do it, but the boss would have my job. She's a real stickler about these things. But I'll tell you what I will do. I will give you a pillow and some blankets and you can pull your car into the parking lot and sleep there."

He disappeared into anther room. I got up to look out the window at my car. I didn't think there was any way I could sleep in that sport, little car.

"Your car is kind of small, but if you're tired enough you can fall asleep anywhere."

He loaded me up with a pillow and several blankets. I must have looked pretty glum because he added, "I guess I shouldn't be telling you this, but they never lock up the church. It won't be warm, but it won't be cold. If from what I see every Sunday is any measure, people can sure fall asleep in those pews."

I started out the door. Then I remembered myself. "I'm sorry. I don't even know your name. Mine's Kate."

"Mine's Tony, Kate."

"Thanks, Tony," I said indicating the pillow and blankets. "I'll return them in the morning."

I trudged out to the car, loaded it up, and pulled the car into the parking area. I leaned my seat back as far as it would go. I couldn't really stretch out. I wrapped the blankets around me and tried to fall asleep. I was bone tired. I would find a comfortable position and settle down. In a few minutes some part of me would start to ache. Then I would shift position, get comfortable, and a few minutes later another part would start to ache. I was so tired I wanted to cry. If I could only stretch out I would be okay.

The church. The first time I thought about it I tried another position. My legs were aching so badly I was desperate. I got out of the car and tiptoed over to the road with my arms full of pillow and blankets. I don't know why I was tiptoeing around. I was probably the only one awake in the whole town. There was just something about sneaking into a church in the dead of night. I looked over at the church. It looked kind of small for all the big doings Tony described. There was a light on over the doorway. After looking up and down the road I hugged my blankets, sprinted for the church, flung the door open, and closed it behind me.

I was in. There was just enough light so I could make my way around. It was much warmer than my car. A soft glow came through double doors across the room. I thought that must be the sanctuary so I headed in that direction.

When I stepped through the doors the sight stunned me. There was a huge cross against the far wall. They had left a backlight on. In the darkened room the glowing cross appeared to be floating. I heard myself say, "My God." I did not know whether to run or to cry so I sat down in the nearest pew.

I do not know how long I sat there contemplating the cross. Eventually, I propped my pillow in a corner of the pew and lay down so I could still see the cross. The last thing I remember thinking before I fell asleep was, "I love Eric and the girls so much. My God, what have I done?"

It was a long table. A meal was spread over the table. Men sat around the table eating and talking. I sat at one end not saying much, joining in a nervous way, feeling somewhat apart, but wanting to belong. I ate some fruit and some unleavened bread dipping the bread in some wine.

Suddenly, something was at my feet. I pulled away and looked down. He looked up at me. His eyes, so kind, the nervousness left me. My body relaxed. I heard Him say, "Please, Judas, allow me to do this for you."

How could I ever refuse Him anything? I gave Him my feet. His touch unleashed a wave of emotion; a glow of warmth and tenderness that is indescribable. He finished with me and moved on without saying any more.

I could not take my eyes from Him. Whether I ate or drank I know not. He instructed us. I tried to listen, but the sight of Him was enough for me. Then I heard Him say, "There is a devil in one of you."

I rose with the others and yelled, "Not me." His words came back to me then. "Please, Judas," He had said. I sank in my seat. Jesus came over to me. A moment before I could not take my eyes from Him. Now I did not want to look into those eyes. I managed to ask, "Master, is it I?"

I forced myself to look at Him. The eyes were still so kind. He nodded and touched me on the head. I wept.

The dinner broke up. All of us went down the stairs and into the road. Jesus with the rest of the disciples headed off together. I waited and watched. I watched until I could no longer see them. Standing in the road there were people all around me, but I was totally alone.

My feet carried me into the city. I had no idea where I was headed until I reached the temple. It was grand, magnificent. Did I hesitate to admire it? No, I barged into the temple where a guard grabbed me and hauled me before the chief priest.

The priest tossed me a bag, which I opened. Silver coins I counted, thirty in number. "Where is he?" he demanded.

I answered, "Follow me." Turning I led them out of the temple.

I had no idea where I was going, but my feet were sure. A great number of armed men followed. I entered the garden at the head of this crowd. I saw Jesus. For the first time I hesitated. Jesus looked at me. I thought, "It's going to be all right." I ran to Him and kissed Him on the cheek.

A tumult broke out. I was cast aside. In minutes Jesus had been led away and the garden was empty. I was alone again. It was unbearable. I ran after the crowd. Before I led, now I trailed after.

We were back in the temple. I hid in a corner. Jesus stood in the center of the room surrounded by priests and elders. Surely they would see what I saw in Him. They led Him out. I crumpled in the corner from exhaustion.

Sounds woke me. I pulled myself to peer around a post. It was a scene similar to the night before. Jesus, bound, was in the center. Around Him were priests and elders. A sentence was read. The priests and elders in their turn indicated acceptance. It was to be death.

Jesus' back was to me as they led Him away. Was I never to look on that face again? Would He not turn to gaze in my direction to let me know I was forgiven? My God, what have I done? He was gone. I burst from my hiding place and flung the bag of coins at the high priest. Falling on my knees I wailed, "I have spilled innocent blood."

The high priest answered, "What is that to us?"

I searched the room for a spark of compassion. I found only hard eyes. They turned away to go about their business. I ran from the temple into the light of day.

The sun was too much to bear. I covered my eyes in pain. There were people everywhere. They were all looking at me. They must all know what I had done. I ran to get away. The eyes followed me. They were looking into me. On I ran. A squad of soldiers marched toward me. They must be coming to kill me. I deserved it. I ducked into a stable to hide. The soldiers marched past. Someone else was coming. I climbed into the loft. They were looking for me. I knew it. There was a rope hanging over a beam. I could put my head through the loop and step off the edge. No one would see me then. I slipped my head through the loop and stepped into air.

I let out a yell that stopped when I hit the floor. An old man was standing over me. "Are you alright he said. "I didn't see you there. I didn't mean to frighten you." He helped me to my feet.

I was still in a daze, uncertain where I was. I looked around and there was the cross. It came back to me now. I was in church. It was the day before Easter I had dreamed I was Judas, a nightmare really. I shuddered at the thought. Then I remembered His face as he looked up at me and said, "Please, Judas …." It had been a dream, but the love I had felt was for Him was real. The despair I felt when I saw Him walk away, condemned, to never see Him again. How could I do that to someone I loved? I was so confused.

The man continued to apologize without me really hearing him. Somewhere in there I heard an offer of coffee and told him, "Yes, please."

The man returned shortly. He handed me a hot mug of coffee. It felt good to hold between my hands. He sat down in the next pew with his own mug. We sat there in a companionable silence waiting for the coffee to cool. A few sips started to wake me up. I looked around the church. "It's much bigger than it looks from out side," I said.

"Yes, I think the architect just hit on the right proportions here. There is a feeling of majesty without being big. There's a warmth here, especially when the building's full."

I took couple of swallows of coffee. I was feeling better by the second.

"Big doings tomorrow," the man said.

"I'm sorry. What are you talking about?"

"Tomorrow is Easter. Aren't you here for the concert tomorrow?"

"No, I'm just passing through. The lodge across the street didn't have any rooms so the night man suggested I could stretch out over here."

"Tony?"

"Yes, I think that's his name."

He smiled and shook his head. "That Tony," he said, "he is a good man, but I don't know where he got the idea of sending people over here to sleep. Every year we have a dozen or so on Saturday night."

We were quiet then. My mind drifted back to the dream, an amazing dream. Why had I dreamed it?

"Do you know what I think about every Easter?" the man asked me. I didn't think I cared. He was not waiting for an answer. "I think of Judas." I shivered when he said this. "Can you imagine what it must be like to be separated from the one you love and to be the cause of that separation?" It felt like a knife plunging into my stomach. "It must be Hell, all over thirty pieces of silver."

"Are you sure that's all there was?" I asked him. "I always thought he was jealous or ambitious."

"It is written that there was a devil in him, but I always thought the devil was the desire for money. Otherwise why even have that in there. No, I think it was placed there to warn us of the dangers of letting money come between us and what we love."

I felt the tears trickle down my cheeks. I waited in silence knowing he would go on. "The funny thing is," he said, "the thing that always gets me is that what he did was so necessary."

"Now you've gone too far," I told him. "How can you say that what he did was necessary? It led to the crucifixion."

"And to the resurrection," he answered.

I was excited now. My voice rose when I said, "How can you say that? There's no way that Judas could have loved Jesus. There's no way anyone who loved someone could do what he did. He couldn't have loved Jesus."

There was silence before he said in a quiet voice, "How could he not love Him? Sometimes we humans just get confused."

I collapsed, my head in my hands. Tears poured forth. My friend got up from his pew and approached. His hand went out to comfort me. I would have welcomed the touch of another human, but he hesitated. Instead he knelt beside me. "I am sorry if I upset you. I am just an old man with crazy ideas. Forgive me?"

I controlled myself and wiped my eyes. "There is nothing to forgive," I told him. "I have other, well, problems. I think it was those problems that upset me. Talking to you just helped me get it out of my system."

He smiled when I said that. Getting off his knees he pointed to my empty cup. "Can I get you more coffee?" he asked.

"No, thank you. It was good coffee."

He took the cup and started away. Stopping he turned to say, "I hope your problems work out. I wish you the very best in your life."

I thought that was an odd thing to wish a stranger. I turned to thank him, but the door to the sanctuary was already closing.

I did have problems to work out. At work I was so good at solving problems, running from one fire to the next. Why was this so different? And so, I sat there, working my problem over and over in my mind. Slowly I noticed the warm glow the sanctuary had in the morning sun. Somehow I stopped worrying about my problem. I just enjoyed being where I was.

A man appeared in the front of the church carrying a stack under each arm. He went through the choir area spreading them around. He turned, looked surprised, and headed in my direction. He was still someway off when he yelled, "You there! You don't belong here. Who are you?"

I did not get a chance to answer. He came right up to me, shaking his finger at me, and said, "You don't belong here. Go on! Get out of here! Go home where you belong!"

I had been feeling good. Now this man made me feel guilty for being there. I gathered up the blankets and pillows and started for the door. I was just opening the door to leave when he said, "Go on! Go home where you belong!"

It struck me. That was the answer. Go home where I belong. I turned to face the man. I smiled. "Thank you," I told him.

Without looking back I marched over to the lodge. I thanked them for the loan of the pillows and blankets. I got into my car and raced back to Eric and the girls. Well, maybe raced is the wrong word. I had too much to live for.

I was Lost

I was lost. I was racing down a two lane blacktop somewhere near the Arizona – New Mexico border. It was almost midnight on Christmas Eve. I did not know where I was and I had no idea what I was doing there.

The details of getting lost were pretty straightforward. I had gotten off the interstate to get gas. The attendant and I started up a conversation. When he heard where I was headed that night he recommended a shortcut that would save over an hour. It seemed simple enough. I took the next exit, traveled two miles, and turned left. The next turn was supposed to be ten to fifteen minutes away and I had been traveling over thirty minutes. I could either turn around and try to find my way back or I could keep going in the same direction until I ran into something. On the horizon there was a faint glow suggesting there might be a town up ahead. I put the high beams back on and put the pedal down.

What I was doing there was another question. I was going to think about 'that day' again. I had lived with 'that day' for over five years. I had reviewed what happened and answered questions about it over and over again. I was out here to forget it, but a thought enters my consciousness and all the memories come flooding back.

I had been an obstetrician in a small city for over twenty-five years. The day had started out just like any other day. One of my mothers had called about nine a.m. thinking she might be in labor. It was nearing her due date so I suggested she go over to the hospital where the nurses in labor and delivery could check on her.

I reviewed the chart. A twenty-five year old with a family history of diabetes, but the blood sugar had been normal throughout the pregnancy. Blood pressure was up over baseline, but the change was not much and salt restriction appeared to keep that under control. A little more weight gain than I liked, but the weight gain was not extreme. The ultrasound was normal. The head was in good position for delivery at the last exam. It had been a routine pregnancy.

An hour later I got the call from the delivery room nurse. The contractions were few and far between. The nurse did not feel it was labor. The delivery room was slow that day so I suggested that they keep her around and do periodic checks anyway. I would be over in an hour.

An hour and fifteen minutes later I said hello. The contractions were not very frequent, but it was clear the mother-to-be was having pain. The nurse told me the baby's heart rate was good throughout a contraction. I listened to the baby's heart rate and palpated the abdomen during a contraction. The baby's heart rate was good. The contraction was strong. The internal exam revealed only a three centimeter dilation of the cervix. It was going to be a long day, but we would keep her.

I headed for the record room to complete some charts. When I got back the nurses informed me that the contractions were more frequent. I suggested putting on a monitor.

I hung out in the doctor's lounge watching the tracings go by. There was no problem. It was just routine. Then I received a call from a nurse. My patient's water had broken. It looked like meconium staining. I ought to come in right away. When I got there it was indeed meconium staining. The presence of meconium said that the fetus had a bowel movement. It can be a sign of fetal distress. We watched the monitor. The heart rate was rock solid. An internal exam showed only five centimeter of cervical dilation. I reassured the parents and headed for the lounge to think and watch the monitor.

I was thinking of doing a c-section. I knew what a disappointment that would be to the parents. Then I watched as the fetal heart rate fell during the next contraction. I rushed back into the room. I had the nurse place the mother on oxygen. The heart rate remained stable during the next few contractions, but then it plummeted once again. I started the process for an emergency c-section and went in to talk to the parents. I told them we had no choice. Even if they did not understand, they accepted my recommendation.

The nurses had never bothered to do the admission paperwork on my patient. We blasted through to the c-section anyway, but I am sure it left the father a bit confused to be doing paperwork while his wife was having a c-section. We got the baby out. The Apgar scores were horrible. Just when you feel like cursing at the top of your lungs you have to be your most professional. I still had another life in my hands.

As soon as I finished the c-section I went over to check on the baby. She was a pretty little thing just over six pounds. They were all pretty to me. She was struggling to breath. The father was there. I told him his wife was in recovery and doing well, the neonatologists were excellent, and how I hoped things would turn out well for his daughter. It did not seem enough to say.

I went back to check the chart. Was there something the nurses had not told me? Was there something I had missed? It was bad enough that it had happened this time, but I did not want it to happen again if I could help it. No, there was nothing. I filed the chart and headed home. I knew I would revisit all this in my dreams for nights to come.

I followed the course of the baby over the next two weeks. As expected she had an aspiration pneumonia. At first she got worse and then, as children often do, turned the corner and was better overnight. The parents were so happy to take their daughter home.

I sat down with the mother a few days after the delivery. I just wanted to tell her how sorry I was that things had not turned out better. No one wanted his 'mothers' to have healthy children more than I did.

I had the expected rough nights trying to figure out whether there was something else I should have done. I never came up with anything. That day receded into the background of a busy life until almost two years later I received notice that I was being sued. The little girl was disabled. The parents were suing me for malpractice.

Over the next two years I reviewed the chart for the insurance company, I reviewed the chart for the lawyers, and I reviewed the chart for the lawyers again. Every night I reviewed the chart, the entire day, in my dreams. I would wake up wondering what I could have done different, wondering what I had done that placed my career and my family in jeopardy. I would go down stairs and watch television or read until I was so tired I could fall asleep. The days were not as bad. I could keep busy. The nights were not so bad when I had to go into the hospital to do a delivery.

About a year into the malpractice suit my wife Annie asked for a divorce. Annie and I had met in college. We had gotten married in medical school. I probably was not much of a husband. Being a good doctor was more important to me. The way I interpreted being a good doctor meant too many soccer games and band concerts missed, too few vacations, and too many nights Annie slept alone. Now, the way I was handling the malpractice suit was too much for her. I did not blame her at all.

The divorce went quickly. When our children, Jennifer and Jason, had gone to college we had opened up a shop in town for Annie to run. The shop was turning a nice profit so Annie refused any alimony. The division of property was fair. The lawyers on both sides wanted to argue, but Annie just wanted to be free from the pain and I did not want to give her anymore.

The date for the malpractice case drew near. The plaintiff had found a technicality for moving the venue for the trial to another county.

My attorney had informed me the new county had a bad reputation for malpractice cases.

The trial date came. On the first day I saw my patients for the first time in years. The child was in some specially rigged carriage. The mother would not even look at me. The father looked at me with hate. I did not really blame the parents. They were looking for money to help their disabled child, looking out for the child's best interests. In this case the two sides would not even be arguing about the same issue. The plaintiff would try to find some technicality that would allow the jury to award compensation. The defense would be defending my reputation. As a doctor no one wanted to see that poor little child get the best care more than me, but why did my reputation need to be trashed to do it?

I even understood the hate. When something unfortunate like this happens there is a tendency to place blame. How can God be so unfair? It is awfully hard to live with that. Was there something you did to make this happen? It is hard to live with guilt for life. It must be someone else's fault. And the more hate the more at fault they are.

The experts for the plaintiff were fairly weak. Nothing they testified to would be a major problem. Then lightening struck. An ink specialist testified that there was an entry in the nursing notes that had been made with a different pen than the others. The ink was the same as I had used in the doctor's notes. The nurse who had written the notes denied that she had written this entry and a nurse from night shift related how I had gone over the chart that night.

There was the case, a forger against a disabled child. The entry was not crucial. I do not know why anyone would have bothered to add it. I certainly had not.

The rest of the case went as expected. My experts were sound. My testimony went well. I was dreading the cross examination, but it was fairly brief. The case went to the jury.

Annie had been there throughout the trial. I never asked why. I just said thank you. She waited with me for the verdict. We talked but not about anything important.

The verdict came. It was a large award for the plaintiff. My attorney talked about appeal. Annie said she was sorry. I was in a daze. Somehow I found my way home to my apartment. Strangely enough, I slept through the night for the first time in a long time.

The malpractice case had not affected my practice. I was as busy as ever. The verdict did not seem to change things. The cost of my malpractice insurance skyrocketed. The waiting list for an appointment was as long as ever. In a few months, when I had gotten over the shock, I started to notice things about the way I practiced. Anything that went wrong instead of being a problem to overcome had become a threat. I realized I was ordering more tests just to be careful. I used to love my patients. Perhaps love is too strong a word, but I thought I had a special connection with my patients. Now, what? I didn't know. It was just different.

The worse part was that practicing obstetrics no longer held any joy for me. That was a shock. I could still remember the first baby I delivered. I was on my first clinical rotation in medical school. It was at a city hospital. A foreign resident with a thick accent poured abuse on me as I delivered my first child. It was such a rush. I had found the key that unlocked me. I had found a career. For over thirty years and over 6,000 deliveries, delivering babies had been a source of joy. I decided to get out.

I sold the practice cheap to a pair of local obstetricians. I sold the office to an ophthalmologist. I did not even bother to renew my medical license when it came up for renewal. I was going to take some time off.

There I was alone in my apartment without any responsibilities facing the holidays. I had always loved Christmas at home with Annie, Jennifer, and Jason. This year was going to be too sad for me to stay. I decided to see America. And, as it was winter I headed south in my old Beamer with a suitcase, a backpack, and a sleeping bag stowed in the trunk.

Now, as I jammed my car along a remote road, my world confined to the illumination of my headlights, the memories of that day and everything that followed plagued me. It was my memory that got me into medical school and got me through medical school. My memory was a major part of what I was. But I would so like to forget.

There was a flash ahead of me. It came again. The memories had distracted me from the road. I stood on the brakes not knowing what to expect. My car screeched to a stop. A young man stepped into the headlights. He held up his hands showing a flashlight, but no weapon. He came to the driver side window. I hesitated. He stood there waiting for me to decide. I heard him say, "Please." I rolled the window down part way.

"Please, sir," he said, "my wife is having a baby. My truck would not start. Do you have one of those cell phones so I can call an ambulance?"

I had left my cell phone at home. "Did you say your wife is having a baby?"

"Yes, sir."

"Where is she? I don't have a phone, but maybe I could drive her to the nearest hospital."

He pointed off to the left. "She is up that hill in a shelter."

"Let me get the car out of the way and then you show me," I told him.

I pulled the car as far over onto the shoulder as I could. I got out and locked up. "How long have you been down here trying to flag down a car?" I asked him.

"About 30 to 40 minutes, you were the first car to come along," he said.

"You left your wife alone for 40 minutes while she was in labor?" I asked him.

"It is okay. She has a rifle," he responded.

It was not the answer I was expecting. The young man headed off the road and up what appeared in the night to be a rather steep hill. Off to one side I saw an old pickup. In fact, I saw it much better than I would have expected for after midnight. I looked up for the first time after getting out of my car and was shocked at what I saw. I had never paid much attention to the night sky having spent most of my life in cities. I was always an eyes on the road type guy. Now I was seeing for the first time the sky in all its glory. I had never seen so many stars. I could even see the Milky Way.

The young man had put some distance between us as I paused admiring the sky. I looked after him, catching the light from his flashlight on the ground. Over his head there appeared to be a star brighter than the rest. Something in the back of my mind stirred reminding me that Venus was the brightest light. But Venus was an evening or morning star. Could it be out after midnight? I did not know.

The young man was getting too far ahead. "Wait for me," I called out to him. He turned and waited while I scrambled up the hill.

When I reached him I held out my hand. "My name is Carter," I said.

He took my hand. "My name is Joseph. It isn't far, now."

Joseph led around one more boulder. There I found a campsite with a fire burning down well surrounded by rocks. There was a blanket hanging against the hillside in front of us between two wooden poles with light coming from around the blankets edge. A low moaning sound seemed to be coming from behind the blanket. Joseph walked up to the blanket with me close behind. Pulling the blanket aside he said, "This is my wife, Maria."

Perhaps I should have been more shocked by the coincidence of names, but all I saw was a woman in pain. There was a lantern beside her. In the illumination I saw a face racked with the pain of a contraction. I knelt beside her and felt her abdomen. The contraction was strong.

"I am a …," I hesitated. What was I? I had no office. I had no medical license. I looked at the face of Maria. My hand lay on her abdomen. The contraction was still strong. The pain was obvious. "I am a doctor," I said.

Maria did not seem to understand. The contraction was easing off. I told her again, but she gave no indication that she understood.

"She does not understand English very well," Joseph said. "I will tell her."

Joseph rattled off something in Spanish. Maria turned to me and smiled. I do not remember whether she was pretty, but I'll remember that smile until I die.

I checked her abdomen now that it was not rock hard from the contraction. The baby seemed to be in good position. I would have given anything for a Doppler so I could check the baby's heart rate. I could not see the baby's head yet and I did not feel comfortable doing an internal exam without gloves or disinfecting my hands. Another contraction began. I had Joseph tell Maria to squeeze my hand and breath like I did. I produced my best imitation of a Lamaze father. Maria caught on fairly quickly. She even smiled again when the contraction was over.

I looked around the little cave. There was not enough light to be sure what they had there. I knew what I had in my suitcase. I pulled out my keys and handed them to Joseph. "Run down to my car and get my suitcase and sleeping bag," I told him. "Hurry! We don't have much time."

I went back to Maria. The contractions were coming frequently now. I did not see the baby's head. It could not be much longer.

Joseph showed with the suitcase. I opened it. I laid out a clean shirt in front of Maria. I found some scissors and cut another shirt into strips. There were some alcohol pads left over from the office. I wiped down the scissors and sterilized my hands as best I could. There was a flashlight in there. I trained it on Maria.

We were just in time. A few big pushes and we'd have a baby. I told Joseph what I wanted Maria to do. He translated. I saw Maria nod. She had a tight grip on both his hands. The contraction came. I yelled, "Now!" Joseph said something. Maria grunted with the effort. The contraction passed. The baby was close. Please be an easy one. Don't get stuck. Not here. Not now.

Another contraction came. Maria was already pushing. The head came, then the shoulders. It was a boy. He had a good cry. His color seemed good. I placed the baby on one of my clean shirts. I tied off the chord and cut it. After wrapping the boy in the shirt I handed him up to Maria. "Congratulations, Joseph, you're the father of a beautiful baby boy." For the first time since he stopped me on the road I saw him smile. Then they kissed.

I finished up with the rest of the delivery no one ever talks about, something I had done thousands of time. When I was satisfied Maria was not bleeding I stood up and almost passed out. I had been kneeling for over half an hour. The rush of the delivery was wearing off. I had gotten up at six the previous morning. Now it was after one. I needed some sleep. The cave was getting chilly. I unzipped the sleeping bag. Looking around for someplace to stretch out my eye caught Joseph, Maria, and the baby. I spread the sleeping bag over them. Maria smiled.

I dug a couple of sweaters out of my suitcase. There was a place where I might sleep sitting up. I settled in and fell asleep in seconds, a dreamless and deep sleep.

I woke up to the sounds of a crying baby, light filtering into the cave around the edge of the blanket. The babe cried again. I tried to get up. I was stiff all over. Moving slowly I crawled to my feet. I checked the baby and mother. Both were doing fine. Maria gave me another smile.

Pulling back the blanket I stepped out side. The morning was cold and crisp with a sky so clear and blue it made you feel like you could see forever. Joseph was bent over the fire. He glanced back at me. A few seconds later he placed a cup of hot coffee in my hands. I gave him a thank you and looked around for a place to sit.

I sat there watching Joseph. I did not know what to say so I sat there in silence. The smell of cooking food filled the air. After awhile Joseph took something into the cave. A few minutes later came back empty handed. Joseph poured himself a cup of coffee and sat down opposite me. There were a few more minutes of silence as he contemplated his cup of coffee. Finally, Joseph broke the silence. "I am sorry, but I only have enough food for my wife," he said.

I gestured with the cup of coffee. "Don't worry about it," I told him.

There was another silence before Joseph said, "We are legal, you know."

It was not exactly what I was thinking about. The subject was obviously important to him so I waited to hear the rest of it.

"I was born here. My father died when I was young. My mother died a few years ago. After my mother died I went to southern Mexico to visit my relatives. That was when I fell in love with Maria. We were married. I came back here to work and Maria came with me. She has a green card."

Joseph stopped. I think he expected me to express some doubts. I changed the subject. "I think Maria is up to traveling,' I said. "We ought to get in my car and head to the nearest hospital so that Maria and the baby can be checked."

"No!"

Joseph said that with a little more emotion than I thought it warranted. "Why?" I asked.

Joseph hesitated before he said, "You said you are a doctor. Tell me that my wife or baby are in danger and I will take them."

I glanced in the direction of the cave. Mother and child were doing great. I was not going to lie to convince him. I changed the subject again. "Have you and Maria thought of a name for your son."

At this Joseph smiled. "Yes," he said, "Maria wants to call him Jesus in honor of the day of his birth."

I smiled at this, too. Jesus, Mary, and Joseph on Christmas Day, I looked up at the blue, blue sky and thought, "Hard to beat that."

For the first time that day I looked at my watch. It was almost noon. I did not feel right leaving Maria and the baby without transportation. Thinking about transportation made me think about my car. I thought I ought to go down the hill to make sure the car was okay.

I told Joseph, "I'm going to check on my car, but I'll be back."

Heading down the hill I kept thinking about Jesus, Mary, and Joseph on Christmas Day. Halfway down the hill I just broke out laughing. I was feeling good, better than I had felt in years.

When I got to my car I was brought up short. A sheriff's cruiser was pulled up behind my car with its' lights flashing. The deputy was standing on the driver's side talking into a microphone. When he saw me he flinched.

I called out, "Can I help you, officer?"

The deputy put the microphone down and approached. "This your car?" he asked.

"Yes, it is," I told him. "The registration and insurance card are in the glove compartment, but I have my driver's license in my wallet. Would you like to see them?"

"Driver's license first," he said.

I took out my wallet and fished out the license. He came close enough to take it from me. While he looked over my license I looked over him. He was young, probably early twenties. I could not tell much else behind the uniform, hat, and glasses. He was close enough I could make out his nametag. He was Deputy Shepherd. I smiled and shook my head.

"This you, Carter?" he asked.

"Well, the picture is about ten years old. I have a lot more gray hair now," I said, " and I could use a shave, but that's me."

"Now the registration."

I walked around to the other side of the car. After unlocking the door I reached in and retrieved the registration without getting into the car. I turned around to hand the deputy the registration. The deputy was right behind me. After taking the registration from me, he ordered me not to move. He went back and sat in his cruiser. I leaned back against the car and waited.

Ten minutes later Deputy Shepherd got out of his cruiser. He came over to me and handed back the license and registration. Then he asked, "Carter, what are you doing out here?"

I told him about the shortcut. When I reached the part about not finding the turn the deputy actually smiled saying, "That road's been closed for three months."

Then I told him about Joseph flagging me down, about Maria, and about delivering her baby.

The deputy walked down the road a piece where he could see Joseph's truck. When he came back he said, "You say you delivered the baby"

I nodded a reply. "You some kind of medic?"

"Something like that," I said.

"How old are Joseph and Maria?" the deputy asked.

"Joseph looks to be about twenty-five and Maria about twenty," I said.

"They sound like the couple that everyone is looking for," the deputy said. "A couple of nights ago some drunks decided it would be funny to scare them. They ended up setting a fire that burned up the couple's trailer. The couple ran out of their trailer, got into their truck, and took off. The trailer was a total loss. No one seemed to know what happened to the couple and the woman was about due."

"What happened to the drunks?" I asked.

"They're in custody," he said. "They should do some time."

I nodded my approval. Deputy Shepherd started walking toward the hill. I trailed after him. "Where are you going, deputy?"

"I'm going up there and take that couple and their baby into the hospital."

"Wait, please?" I asked him.

The deputy stopped and turned. I caught up with him. "I know your intentions are good, but how would you feel if you were burned out and probably harassed before that and now a sheriff's deputy orders them into town in the back of his cruiser? Pretty humiliating. What happens if they don't want to go with you? Your authority will be challenged. You'll try to force them. And when they get to the hospital what do they do, where do they live?"

Deputy Shepherd did not say anything. He nodded slightly in agreement. He continued looking up the hill trying to decide.

"I don't know whether they are breaking any laws, but it is Christmas. Let's not turn them into criminals unless we have to. Let me go back up there and try to talk them down. If they are not out of there by tomorrow morning, you do what you have to."

Deputy Shepherd took one more look up the hill. He turned back to his cruiser. As he walked toward his cruiser he said, "I'm heading into town. I'll report this when I get there. You better have them out of here by tomorrow morning. And get this piece of junk off my road by tonight. I don't want anybody running into your car in the middle of the night."

I followed the deputy to his cruiser. He got in and started the engine. I knocked on the window before he could drive away. Deputy Shepherd cracked the window. "Merry Christmas, deputy," I told him. I think he even smiled as he drove away.

Pregnant and burned out of your home a couple of nights before Christmas, it explained what they were doing out here. It, also, explained the anger I felt in Joseph.

For the first time that day I was feeling hungry. I had a box of cookies and some energy bars in my car. I grabbed the cookies and energy bar along with a bottle of water and headed up the hill. When I got to the camp there was no one around. I thought they were probably in the cave behind the blanket. I found a nice rock to sit on and broke into the cookies. I had eaten quite a few when I realized that Maria and Joseph probably did not have enough to eat. I approached the cave and called, "Hello in there." Joseph came out in a little while. He looked surprised that I was still there. I held out the box of cookies and energy bars to him.

"Some food for you and your wife. I had it in the car and I've already had enough. Please, take some."

Joseph hesitated. Finally, he took the food. He said, "Thank you," and disappeared behind the blanket. I headed back to my rock.

It was a gorgeous day. The sky was a deep blue. I tried to figure out how many distinct shades of blue there were from the horizon to the zenith. I was feeling really good about myself, better than I had felt in years. The thought crossed my mind that I should be trying to convince Joseph to come with me into town, but for first time in a long time I had faith that things would work out. If I waited long enough something good would happen.

I had spent about two hours enjoying the day when I saw three men starting up from the bottom of the hill. I thought I should meet them halfway. When I got close enough I stuck out my hand and said, "Hello, my name is Carter."

In certain circles such a gesture necessitates introductions. We all shook hands. One was Roy, the president of the Kiwanis. Augusto was president of the Rotary. John was president of the Lions.

Once the introductions had been made, Roy started out, "We understand that you had a child delivered out here."

"That's right,' I said, "a Christmas baby, a nice six and a half pound boy, mother and child doing fine."

"That's wonderful," Roy said. "You've heard about the fire?" I nodded.

"Terrible thing to happen just a couple of weeks after Joseph lost his job when the meat plant closed. Close to a hundred jobs lost, that's a lot for a little town like ours. Still, we would have helped them if they hadn't taken off after the fire. People have been looking for them ever since. We'd like to help them now. John here has an apartment he would let them have for awhile."

John broke in, "It's not too big, but it's clean. There's a refrigerator and stove that work. A washer and dyier are just down the stairs. We might even be able to work out something long term with him acting as super."

Augusto chimed in now, "And I think I have a job for him. It won't pay as much as at the meat plant, but I need dependable workers."

Roy picked it up again, "We have some furniture for the apartment including a bed and a crib. We hit up a couple of local stores for diapers. Those of us who didn't have anything they could give passed the hat. Tens and twenties add up to a few hundred to get them back on their feet. We just want the opportunity to show Joseph and Maria that what happened the other night is not the way the rest of the town thinks." There were nods of agreement all around.

"Joseph and Maria are camped up the hill here," I told them. "We'll go up there, but let me talk to Joseph first. He's pretty angry about what happened the other night. Follow me."

I headed toward the camp with the three presidents in tow. When we were in view of the cave I told them, "Wait here."

Pulling the blanket slightly aside I called in, "Joseph, I need to talk to you. I'm coming in."

When I stepped inside Joseph was getting to his feet. I started right in, "There are three men out there from the town. They would like to speak with you and I think you should listen."

"No," Joseph said, "I will not talk to anyone from that town."

"Listen, Joseph. I know about the fire and your job. A deputy sheriff told me that the people who burned your trailer are in jail. These men want to offer you a job. They've got a place for you to stay with a bed and a crib. They even have some money to tide you over."

"You don't understand. I can't take their charity. You weren't there when they burned our trailer."

"No, I wasn't. Neither were these men. They seem like good men, responsible men. They left their families on Christmas day to find you. Sometime you will realize what a sacrifice that is. Besides, you will be giving them something in return."

"What have I to give them?" Joseph asked.

"Forgiveness."

Joseph nodded. Forgiveness he understood because it was going to take an effort for him to forgive. He looked at his wife and child. Maria sat there smiling. The baby slept peacefully in her arms. "I will listen to these men," Joseph said.

"Good. I will get them. If they want you to go with them, go. I will clean up here and put everything in your truck. I'm sure they will help you find someone to help start your truck tomorrow. Things will work out."

I left Joseph and Maria and returned to the three men. "Joseph and Maria will see you now. Joseph is still angry over what happened the other night. Just remember that they are new parents. Make a fuss over the baby and things will be alright."

I made a show of pulling aside the blanket. "Gentlemen, Maria, Joseph, and their baby, Jesus." I pronounced it with a soft 'J.'

The three presidents did not miss a beat. They introduced themselves and asked to see the baby. The compliments started flowing with Joseph translating for Maria. I retreated to my rock.

About fifteen minutes later I heard voices approaching. The three presidents had Maria and Joseph with them.

Roy came by, shook my hand, and said, "We're going to take Maria, Joseph, and the baby into town so they can stay in their new apartment."

Joseph and Maria stopped in front of me. I stood up. Joseph took my hand and said, "Thank you."

Maria moved in closer. She put her hand up as if to touch my cheek. I leaned over slightly. Unexpectedly, she kissed my cheek. Maria rattled off something in Spanish ending with "Thank you," in English.

I looked at Joseph wondering what she had said. Joseph answered, "She says you are a very good doctor."

I just stood there watching until they had disappeared from sight. It was getting late in the day so I started out breaking up the camp. There was not really much to it. I put everything in the bed of the pickup. The last thing I packed was my suitcase. I carried the suitcase down and stowed it in my car. The suitcase did not feel as heavy as the day before.

After grabbing a bottle of water from the car I headed back to my rock to rest. There was nothing holding me there. I could have left as soon as I had packed everything away. I did not want to leave. I always seemed to be running through life, from delivery suite, to office, to operating room, and back around again. Now I had a chance to just be.

The sun was setting. It was a great pleasure just sitting there watching the sky change color. Finally, a star appeared, an evening star. It was probably Venus, I thought.

It had been a special Christmas day. There had been a shepherd, three wise men, and Jesus, Mary, and Joseph. Yes, it was an extraordinary Christmas. I did not know what I was going to do the next day. I had no malpractice insurance. I did not even have a license anymore. I had a profession I love. I was given one last chance to practice it. I looked up at the stars and said, "Thank you."

Why

"Ted, you have to come to our special Christmas concert. With you there it will feel like old times."

Reverend Bob was a nice man. He was just doing his job, visiting us shut-ins. What he could not know was that remembering old times was the problem. Memories would come flooding back.

"Now, I have thought of everything. There are lots of people who would love to drive you to and from the concert," Reverend Bob said. "After the concert we are having an old fashioned pancake supper. It will be a good time. I even promise to keep my sermon short."

"A short sermon is no good," I told him. "How am I supposed to catch up on my sleep?"

"There you go," Bob said. "That's the spirit. We still need you, Ted. I want you to come."

I told him I would think about it. We passed a few more pleasantries as I ushered him out of the front room and to his car. He wished me a merry Christmas. I waved him down the drive. I had thought about it. I would not be going. There would be too many memories. I went back in to the front room and sat down.

I could not get over the memories. Some were still crystal clear after all these years.

I had grown up on a farm just a few hundred miles from the farm I was living on now. I can still remember walking out into the fields on a moon-less night. I would just get beyond the lights of the house and look up at the stars. Once my eyes had adapted to the dark the sky was filled with so many stars it was just incredible. I still do not know how city folk live without that sight. No one in my family had ever gone to college. Why bother? All you really needed was some honest work and there was plenty of that right there on the farm. I think it was those stars calling me that sent me to college.

I got into the state AG school. I had to work two jobs to stay there. Most of the students were learning something about farming. I was not interested in that. I was not sure what I was there for until late in my junior year. I wanted to be a doctor.

I applied to the state medical school. I did not think about going anyplace else. That was 1941. Pear Harbor changed everything. I was able to finish out my college career. I was accepted into medical school, but for the moment I had a higher calling. I graduated one day and reported to the Marines the next.

I had been in for about a year when we attacked a Japanese held island. I had seen some combat, been promoted to corporal, but this was my first landing under fire. We had further to go in the water than what we were told. The water was deeper. We plodded toward the beach. I saw my sergeant take one in the chest. Someone else got hit near me. I grabbed him and hauled him onto the beach.

When I had a chance to look around I realized the lieutenant was nowhere to be found. Someone yelled out, "Corporal, what do we do next?" Supposedly I did all right. I do not remember that day very well. I got a promotion and a couple medals out of what happened that day. I ended up waking up in a hospital a few days later. I always tell people that was why I cannot tell them the details, but I really think I do not remember that day because killing humans was what I had to do, not something to remember.

I got pretty sick. The doctors told me I almost died. I was shipped back to a hospital to recuperate. One day I woke up and there she was. Emily was a vision. I could not get over her. Over a few days we got talking. It turned out she was from a farm just like I was. In fact, her parent's farm was just a few hundred miles from where my parent's farm was. Having the chance to talk to her was just the tonic I needed. I got better fast, too fast. I was discharged from the hospital and had orders to report to a new outfit. Before I left I waited for her outside. I had to be careful, her being a lieutenant and my being only a sergeant. I caught her when she was alone. I told her that when all this was done I was going to medical school and as soon as I was in medical school I was going to find her. Em looked at me like I was crazy. I did not realize that I was proposing in a backhand, middle of a war kind of way. Then she smiled. "I hope you find me, Ted," she said. It was all she had to say. She walked off to catch up with a couple of the other nurses. There was just a quick backward glance with that smile of hers.

I went back to war. I waded ashore a couple of times, but I tried never to do anything heroic. I didn't want my men to do anything heroic either. I thought we had a better chance of killing the enemy if we stayed alive. Still, we did some good fighting and I ended up a lieutenant with some more medals.

I separated from the marines in early '46. The first thing I did was head for the state medical school where I had been accepted back in '42. I talked my way into the dean's office. I think he wanted to tell me that the class was full up. I stood there at attention with a chest full of medals and asked him when I should report. He hesitated and he looked me over. After awhile he stood, reached across the desk to take my hand, and told me, "Classes begin in September. Make sure we have all the updated paperwork." I thanked him and left before he could change his mind.

The next thing I did was look up Em. I took a bus to her hometown. Asking around I was able to find where her family's farm was. I walked out there on a beautiful spring day only to find out she was not there. She was nursing at the state medical school. Her parents were awfully nice. Em had written about me. They gave me a big dinner and then I set out.

I found the apartment Em shared with a couple of other nurses. I don't think I was ever as nervous as I was when I knocked on her door, not even when I waded ashore under fire. We had exchanged a few letters, but none for several months. I did not know whether I had missed the letters or she had found someone new. I should not have worried. She opened the door with that smile of hers. Seeing her made me so weak I thought I was going to fall out. The only thing that kept me upright was Em throwing her arms around me. I had not known until then how much in love she was with me. I knew we had struck a chord in each other. Em was worried that this was just another hospital romance during war. She did not want to make too much out of it. After all, soldiers die.

We decided to get married right away. While she planned the ceremony I went out to find a job. With so many returning soldiers good jobs were hard to find. I found three part time jobs working over eighty hours a week that added up to one good job. I saved enough to start medical school. With Em's salary as a nurse, my part time jobs, and the GI bill I we were able to make it through medical school. Internship might actually have been worse. While I was receiving some pay the amount was low and the hours were so long there was no way I could work part time.

I had planned on specializing, but during internship Em got pregnant. On top of that was the fact that Em's father was ill. She wanted to return home rather than wait through three more years of residency.

We returned to Em's hometown. I hung out my shingle and was busy right away. One of the older GP's had a big OB practice. He was getting tired and wanted to give up the late nights. Luckily, I enjoyed the OB rotation in internship. I was there only a few days before I delivered my first baby. I thought I was pretty good at it. Compared to the standards of today it was seat of the pants stuff. I tried to keep fresh by going back to the medical school for a couple of days of observation each year.

Em delivered a beautiful little girl later that year. We called her Joan after one of Em's aunts. Next year Em was pregnant again. This time there were complications. The baby was lost. Em never got pregnant again. We had wanted a big family. Well, with Joan we had a lot of love.

Em found something to keep her busy. When Joan was old enough for school Em started working in my office. She knew everybody and everybody knew her. She turned my office into one big family.

Joan grew up, got married, and moved away. She would come to visit often enough, but Em missed her. Then Joan had little Ted. I think he was the spitting image of me at that age. Em just loved him so much.

I think little Ted was about ten when it happened. Joan's husband was stuck overseas for Christmas. On Christmas Eve Joan was driving with little Ted to our house for Christmas. An ice storm came up. An eighteen wheeler was going too fast, jackknifed, and tipped over crushing Joan and little Ted.

It was too much for Em. She stopped coming to the office. She spent all her time at the farm her parents had left us. I had a choice. If I wanted to keep my wife I had to give up medicine. It really was not much of a choice. I was old enough to retire. I gave the practice to a young doctor I had just recruited. We sold the house in town. We became farmers.

Em and I had another good five years. Then she became sick. I spent five years being a caregiver again, carting her to specialists, watching her die. The last ten years, well, the last ten years I have existed. Everyone I cared about was dead.

"Hello, Doctor. Are you home?"

Marge, my housekeeper called out from the front door. I do not know why she does that. I am always home. She came to work for me after Em died. Her husband had passed a couple of years before. The job gave her something to do and a little income. I think she always hoped that something more might happen, but to me she's a youngster of only 75. I waved a hello, grabbed my hat and coat, and headed out to the barn to tend the livestock.

The special Christmas concert came and went. Reverend Bob gave me another call, but I did not want to relive old times. I did not do much anymore, a trip a week into town for groceries and a stop at the library. I have a man who does all the real farming. I make a few dollars, but he's got a real nice family so I make sure he gets enough. I have some livestock, but they are more pets than anything else.

Sometime after Em's death I started getting a physical on her birthday, December 22nd. Somehow I've been lucky, no medicines, no problems. Once a year is all I need. I have been seeing Jim Wallace, the young doctor I recruited just before I quit. He must be fifty now.

"Doc, how are you doing?" Jim is the only one who calls me 'Doc' anymore.

"Good to see you, Jim," I answered.

We shook hands and he commenced with the exam. It was my old exam room spruced up a bit. After I had been poked and prodded, had some blood work drawn, Jim said, "I don't know how you do it, Doc. Eighty-five and still healthy as a horse. Whatever it is you should bottle it."

I smiled. I started getting dressed when I asked Jim, "What is it like to practice medicine these days?"

Jim stopped. He thought for a minute. "You'd hate it. There are more rules and regulations than I can keep straight. If I remember right you did a lot of OB. The malpractice premiums are so high I had to drop OB a couple of years ago. You don't know how lucky you are to have gotten out when you did."

Somehow I did not consider myself lucky. Jim went on with his complaints about practicing medicine, but I had tuned out.

Christmas Eve came. I looked around the house. There was nothing Christmas about the house. Later a storm would move in, but now the night was clear and cold. I put on my hat and coat to make a trip I had made a hundred times. I walked out into the middle of a field and looked up. The sky was filled with stars. The night sky had always filled me with awe and wonder. Tonight it reminded me of my youth. It reminded me of the sky I saw from troop ships and south Pacific islands, of nights with Em. The thought of Em was too much. This night was the anniversary of Joan's and little Ted's deaths. The memory of Joan and little Ted crushed in their car hit me with such force I fell to my knees. I cried. I had not cried for years. The tears poured from my eyes. I heard myself ask, "Why am I still here? Why am I still here?" I looked up again and found only silence. The wind blew cold. It was time to head back.

I dragged myself back to the house. Supper was waiting in the kitchen. It would have to wait. I got undressed and into bed. A few minutes later I was asleep.

Something woke me up. I looked at the clock, 1:00 am. It was Christmas. I got up and relieved myself. Before getting back in bed I pulled aside a shade. There was a car there. It was over near the barn. The barn door was open. I watched for a while. An ice storm had blown in since I had gotten in bed. It was pretty brutal out there. I got back into bed. I did not really try to fall asleep. Ten minutes later I got up and looked again. The wind was blowing the rain pretty good. Nothing had changed. I decided to go down there and check it out.

I bundled up well and got the big flashlight. I was a little scared. I thought of bringing weapon with me, but I was eighty-five. If I had a weapon I was the most likely person to be hurt by it. When I stepped outside it was wet and windy and cold. There was no way I could sneak up on the situation. I was going to have to get inside the barn as fast as possible. I had to hope for the best.

I went as fast as I could across the yard into the barn. The wind was whipping up good. After I had closed the door behind me I heard the sound. It was a sound I had heard often before. Someone was in pain.

I turned the flashlight on and found the light switch. When I flipped the switches nothing happened. I cracked the door to the barn and looked back at the house. I was pretty sure I had left a light on, but the house was totally dark. The storm had knocked out the power.

I heard that sound again. I scanned the barn with my flash. The source of the sound was not too far away. I found her lying back on a pile of hay. Her abdomen was huge. She was obviously in the middle of a contraction. I shined the light on my face. She said, "I think I'm going to deliver."

Without even thinking I said, "I'm a doctor."

She took my hand in both of hers and squeezed. In less than a minute the contraction had subsided. She let go of my hand. I checked my hand to make sure it still worked.

"So, what's a nice pregnant girl like you doing in my barn?" I asked her.

"I was trying to make it home for Christmas. I didn't think it was going to be a problem because my due date isn't until next week. Then I started to have contractions. Then my water broke. I thought I was still going to be okay until the ice storm hit. I don't think I did five miles in the last hour. I was scared I would end up in a ditch and my baby and me would freeze to death. I was just trying to make it here."

That surprised me. She started to have another contraction so I gave her the other hand and showed her how to breathe to ease the pain. When the pain stopped I asked her, "Why were you trying to get here?"

"You're Dr. Anderson, aren't you?"

"Well, yes, but how did you know I lived here?"

"You don't remember me. My name is April Waller. You delivered me. My mother is Sherri Johnston Waller," she said.

It took a moment. Finally, I placed the names. "I remember now, Sherri and Bill Waller. So you're April?"

April nodded her head. She was already having another contraction. She started panting. I gave her my other hand to squeeze.

When the pain had passed I told her, "The contractions are too close together. I don't think it will be long now. We have to get you into the house."

I stood up and took her hand. She pulled away. "I can't do it, Dr. Anderson," she said. "When I got out of the car it took everything I had to crawl in here."

"Do you have a cell phone? We could call for help."

"The batteries are dead."

"I'll run over to the house," I told her. "The power lines are down, but maybe the phone lines are working. I'll grab some blankets and things before I come back. I won't be long. I promise."

I ran as fast as I could back to the house. Once in the house I headed for the kitchen. The phone was not working. I had a couple of flashlights stored away. Once I found them I dumped the contents of the laundry basket on the floor. I headed to the upstairs linen closet where I filled the basket with towels and blankets. In my room I threw in a couple of new shirts that I had never gotten around to wearing. In the bathroom I found alcohol and some iodine solution. I was headed back down the stairs when I saw my old doctor's bag. I had not looked inside it for over a decade. I grabbed it and headed down the stairs.

I was almost to the front door when it hit. A crushing chest pain felled me. I was on the floor gasping for breath. "Not now," I said. "Please, not now. Not when someone is depending on me. Please. Please, not now."

The chest pain subsided. I could breathe again. I made it to my feet, loaded up the basket and headed to the barn. I did not dare run now. With every step I said, "Thank you."

Inside the barn I set to work. I got a blanket under April and placed another one over her. April wriggled out of her pants so I could examine her. I poured some alcohol over my hands and rubbed them together. The baby appeared to be in the normal delivery position. The head was almost crowning. It would not be long now. Less than ten minutes later after a couple of big pushes the baby was delivered.

"It is a beautiful little girl," I told her. I wrapped the baby in a towel I had brought and handed her over.

"It's awfully dark in here, but she does look beautiful, doesn't she, "April said.

"Yes, she's a cutie with ten fingers and ten toes. Everything seems to be in working order. Just listen to those lungs."

"It's alright that she's crying now, isn't it?" April asked.

"Don't worry. In your arms she will settle down," I told her.

And just as if the baby could have heard those words she settled in to her mother's arms. That brought a smile to my face. How many times over the years had I witnessed a mother and child together in the moments just after birth? To see it again after all these years seemed like a miracle.

I had a patient after all these years and she was still bleeding. I massaged the abdomen. The uterus seemed to be contracting nicely. The blood continued to come. I soaked it up with towel after towel. I tried to see what the matter was, but the light of the flashlight was too weak. She must have torn something. What I wouldn't do for a decent light and a suture?

"Is everything alright Dr. Anderson?" April asked.

"Well, there's been some bleeding. Sometimes during birth something can tear. If we were in a hospital it would be no problem to sew it up and stop the bleeding. But don't worry. These things stop on their own and it will be no problem to sew it up later when we get you to a hospital," I answered her.

The blood was still coming. I was desperate. I cut one of my cleaned shirts into strips, soaked them in an iodine solution, and packed her as best I could. I felt her pulse. It was weak. I found my old blood pressure cuff and stethoscope. The reading was 90/50.

"We've got to get your legs up and your head lower so that the blood will get to your heart and brain," I said to her.

I set about arranging her position. It was a little awkward with her holding the baby, but I did not want to take the baby away from her.

"Do you feel any better now?" I asked her when we finished.

"I feel cold, Dr. Anderson. Could you hold me?" April said.

I got a blanket and spread it over us as I lay down next to her. She moved against me. I hadn't been this close to another human being in years. I turned off the flashlights to conserve their batteries in case we needed them. We lay there in the dark.

I was used to silence after all these years alone. There was never absolute silence. If you listened carefully, there was always the sound of the wind or, perhaps, an animal moving about. I felt at home with those small sounds.

"Dr. Anderson, what are we going to do?" April asked after awhile.

"Don't you worry," I told her. "I have it all planned out. I left the barn light switch on. If the electric comes on we will know right away. If the lights do not come on I will head out to the road at first light and flag down a truck. They use this road as a cut-through so I imagine there'll be trucks even on Christmas day."

"Are my baby and me going to be alright?" April asked after another period of silence.

"Your baby is going to be just fine," I answered. "You've lost a little blood, but you're young. You'll do fine."

I did not want her asking anymore questions regarding her condition so I changed the subject. "Do you know how special it is to have a Christmas baby?" I asked her.

"Oh, I figure she will hate it. Who wants to share their birthday?" April said.

"I suppose that is true, but I always think of it another way. Christmas is the birth of hope and faith. Just like a newborn hope and faith are miracles. Like a newborn hope and faith need to be nurtured to reach their full potential. I've delivered a dozen or so Christmas babies over the years. Each one, well, every baby was special to me, but the Christmas babies made me feel as if I was living Christmas, each baby a reminder of the one baby born so many years ago. And so it is with your baby. I can't believe that after all these years I've had another chance."

Tears came to my eyes, the second time after so many years. As I wiped them away I noted April shaking. She was sobbing.

"April, please don't pay any attention to me. I am just an old man."

"It isn't you, Dr. Anderson. I just wanted to go home again."

April sobbed. Not knowing what to do, I held her a little tighter being careful of the baby she held. With time the sobbing stopped. I dried her tears and asked her to tell me about it.

"I left a couple of years ago in anger," she began. "I had fallen in love with a man my parents did not approve of. I was living with him when I got pregnant. Last summer I came home to visit. My father could barely say a word to me. My mother was always yelling. I left without telling them I was pregnant. Then my boyfriend left. I was alone and scared. No one loved me. But then I thought you could always go home on Christmas. That's why I was traveling last night. I just wanted to go home."

"But, April, your parents love you. I know them. They'll be so happy to see you and your baby. They won't be able to think of anything else," I told her.

"That's easy for you to say Dr. Anderson. You've never been alone. You've always had someone who loves you. You have a whole town that loves you. Every time one of us would get sick my mother would always say, 'If only Dr. Anderson hadn't retired.' Then she would go on and on about how wonderful you were. She was right, Dr. Anderson. You're pretty wonderful."

I did not feel wonderful. In fact I felt pretty miserable. After all these years I had a patient again. She might be slowly bleeding to death before my eyes, but I was too old and feeble to do much about it. Worse yet, she was in pain. I had no clue what to say or do to ease that pain.

In the quiet of the barn I could make out the sounds the livestock made while sleeping. Then the baby made a sound as if to remind me that she was there. I could not really make out the baby in the dark, but just the thought of her reminded me of Christmas.

"Miracles do happen, April," I said. "If you have any doubts just look at your daughter. It is Christmas. Have faith."

I do not know whether she heard me. Did it help her? I do not know. I know it helped me.

Silence stretched as I tried to stay awake. Mother and daughter were sleeping well. I waited for the first light of dawn.

Something woke me. Despite my efforts I had fallen asleep. I could just make out a weak light from outside. I woke April and told her to be careful with her baby as I had to leave her for a while. I felt April's pulse before I left. It was weak and rapid. She managed a smile as I left.

When I got outside I could just make out the sun breaking the horizon. I went into the house to try the phone. The phone was still out. I found the flares I kept in my old car and headed out to the road.

Just before the entrance to my farm the road comes down a hill and around a curve so that the trucks had to slowdown. I walked up the hill and threw down a lighted flare. I threw another one down on the curve and a third at the entrance to my place. I waited a little further along to flag down anything that came past.

It was cold that morning. I had put on a sweater and my warmest coat, a hat I could pull down over my ears, gloves, and a scarf. I stood there stamping my feet and flapping my arms trying to stay warm, watching the one flare I could see burn down. I had three more flares if those burned out. After that I would have to hope that the trucks were being careful or they might run me down.

The flare burned out. I trudged up toward the curve with my head bent low against the wind. I barely heard it coming what with the wind and my hat over my ears. I looked up just in time to jump in the ditch.

The truck stopped a little further along. The truck driver ran down to where I was struggling to get out of the ditch. He reached down and pulled me up to the road.

"It wasn't my fault," the truck driver said. "I wasn't even speeding. It wasn't my fault."

"No, it wasn't your fault," I told him. "Don't worry about me. There's a young girl in my barn. She gave birth last night. I think she may be bleeding. Do you think you can raise the sheriff on your CB?"

The truck driver looked over at the barn for a moment as if that was going to tell him something. Without saying a word he took off for his truck. I had no doubt that he was heading for his CB. I yelled after him, "Tell them the Anderson place." When he disappeared into his cab I headed back to the barn.

April's eyes were closed as I approached. I picked up her wrist to feel her pulse. Her eyes snapped open. "Dr. Anderson, you were gone so long."

"I didn't want to be. I stopped a truck. The driver is calling the sheriff on his CB. An ambulance should be here in ten minutes. Do you think you can make it?"

"I think so," April said. "I feel so dreamy, like I am only half here. I've been trying to stay awake for the baby, but I keep on going in and out."

"You keep on calling her 'the baby.' Don't you have a name picked out?"

"I had several that I was thinking about. I was going to wait until I saw her to decide. I think I have one picked out now, but I want to wait."

The truck driver showed up. He was panting as if he had run in here from his truck. He stood over us and looked down at April and her daughter.

"I got hold of the sheriff. He's sending an ambulance out right away," he said.

"Hear that April. An ambulance is on its way," I told April. "This is the nice man that stopped and called the sheriff for us. What is your name, sir?"

"My name is Gerald," he answered.

I extended my hand and Gerald took it. "Gerald, my name is Ted. I want to thank you for stopping. This is April and her daughter. April this is Gerald."

"Thank you, Gerald," April said. She managed a smile.

Gerald smiled back. "It is a pleasure, April. Is there anything I can do?"

I could hear a siren in the distance. "Maybe you could wait outside for the ambulance and waive them in here?"

"Good idea," Gerald said. He took one last look at April and her child and headed for the road.

"It won't be long now, April." I squeezed her hand, but there was no response. I looked at her. Her eyes were closed. My fingers went to her throat. There was a pulse, rapid and weak.

The ambulance was entering the barn now. I scooped up the baby and stepped out of the way.

The emergency medical techs were very professional. One of them took one look at me. I just told them, "She's lost a lot of blood. She needs I.V. fluids." He checked her pulse. They transferred her to a stretcher, hooked her up to a monitor, and started an intravenous. Within minutes of their arrival April was loaded into the ambulance and ready to go to the hospital. The last thing one of the EMT's did before they left was take the baby from me. She had started crying as soon as I had taken her from April. Still, it was hard to let her go.

I trailed after the ambulance to the door of the barn. Gerald joined me in watching the ambulance disappear down the road. When at last it was quiet, Gerald asked, "Is she going to be alright? She was so pale, like she didn't have any blood in her."

"Well, she is young. That always helps."

We were quiet, then, just two people enjoying the morning. The storm had washed the clouds away leaving behind a crystal blue sky. The sun dazzled off the ice that had built up on the tree limbs. Soon it would all melt. Now it had a magical quality. It was a good morning to be alive.

Gerald looked at his watch. "I didn't even think about the time," he said. "I'm way behind schedule. Can I give you a lift into town?"

"No, I do not think I can make it right now. I did not get much sleep last night so I think I will go inside, make some breakfast, and have a cup of coffee. I would be happy to make some for you."

"Thanks, but I've got to run. Maybe I'll stop one of the next times I drive past here to see how she did."

"That would be nice. And Gerald, thanks a lot," I called after him.

Gerald was already at the road. He turned around and waived. "No reason for thanks," he said. "It's Christmas."

I watched Gerald start up his truck and head down the road. I was alone again. A flurry of excitement and, well, I should be used to it by now. I thought about that cup of coffee, but the livestock needed feeding. No reason they should go hungry.

There was a banging. I could hear it, but it seemed to be in a dream. It happened again. This time I struggled awake. I was in my easy chair in the front room. A cold cup of coffee was on the table beside me. I glanced at my watch. It was one o'clock. I had slept for nearly five hours. The banging recurred. This time the banging was accompanied by someone shouting, "Hello, is anybody home?"

I pulled myself to my feet. Everything hurt. I shuffled over to the door saying, "I'm coming," a few times on the way.

There was a young deputy sheriff at the door. Holding the door open I asked, "What can I do for you?"

The deputy looked me over. "You Anderson?" he asked.

"Yes, I am Ted Anderson," I replied. "Is there some kind of problem?"

"I wouldn't know anything about that," he said. "The Sheriff just gave me orders to bring you in."

That could mean only one thing. April had died. I fought back tears.

The deputy grew impatient. "It's Christmas. Could you hurry along?" he said.

"Of course, I just have to grab my coat and hat."

I left the door open while I went to the hall closet. When I turned with coat on and hat in hand the deputy had stepped inside. I guess he thought he had to watch me. He ushered me out to his cruiser. He opened the back door. I got in. He closed the door behind me.

It is not a long drive into town, on the short side of five miles. The deputy called in as soon as we hit the road. I heard him say something about picking up Anderson. I could not hear the rest of it well enough to know what he said. The deputy did not say anything to me the rest of the way. For him I was just business. For my part I was still stunned by the loss of April.

When we hit town we drove right past the sheriff's office. We ended up at the emergency entrance to the hospital. The Sheriff was there to greet us. He was smiling.

The Sheriff pulled the door open and offered me a hand out. "Doc, it is good to see you. How long has it been?"

The Sheriff was a big, florid man. He had been a patient way back when. I tried to remember what his problems were. Hypertension, gout and cigarettes came to mind. I think I had convinced him to stop smoking.

"Probably ten or more years, Andy," I told him.

"Way too long," Andy said. "Come on in here. Your patients are waiting for you."

The Sheriff turned to lead the way down a corridor. He went on about the rescue squad and the obstetrician. I was not paying any attention. April was alive. They had not flown her out to the regional medical center so she must be doing okay.

We had gone half the way down the corridor when Sherri Waller, April's mother, came out of one of the rooms. She saw us. Her eyes widened. She ran toward us and threw her arms around me.

"Oh, Doctor Anderson," she said, "how can I ever thank you? My little girl, out there all alone, what miracle brought her to your door? Thank you. Thank you. Thank you."

"April and the baby are okay, then?" I asked.

"Okay? Come over here."

Sherri took my hand and led me over to the nursery. "She's the one on the end. She's perfect and so cute."

We stood there in front of the glass watching another little human sleep. I always enjoyed this moment. It made all the late nights seem worthwhile. Eventually I said, "She is a cutey," just as I have said a thousand times before.

Sherri took my arm and pulled me back toward the room she had been leaving. "Come on. Come on. April has been worried about you."

As we entered the room Sherri announced, "Look who I found."

April was sitting up in bed hooked up to an IV. "Oh my god! Doctor Anderson, are you okay? I was so worried about you having to be up all night and out in the cold. Have you seen Theodora, yet?"

"Theodora?"

April and her mother exchanged a look. "That's right, Theodora. I've decided to name her after you."

"I am honored, but I cannot let you have your daughter stuck with a name like Theodora just because of me."

April waved me off. "Don't worry about it. I've already thought of it. We'll probably call her Dora, but maybe Teddy. I think Teddy is a cool name for a girl."

I thought of that for a second. She was probably right. Teddy might be a cool name for a girl now.

I turned a doctor's eye on April. She looked a lot better than when I last saw her, but her color was still off. She was excited now. Pretty soon she would crash.

"You look a lot better than the last time I saw you," I said. "How do you feel?"

"They gave me two bottles of that IV stuff. After that I was feeling a lot better. I still feel a little lightheaded. The obstetrician said that might take a few days to go away. They didn't have to give me any blood though he said it was close. He said you did exactly the right thing."

A nurse brought in little Theodora. I was surprised that she had brought the baby in with everyone there. Bill Waller, April's father, showed up right after the nurse left. He came right over and shook my hand.

"Dr. Anderson, I can't thank you enough," he told me while pumping my arm. "I owe you for all three of my girls, three generations of Waller girls."

April became excited. "Oh, that's right," she said. "You delivered Mom. You delivered me. And now you delivered Theodora. We need a picture. We need a picture. Dad, did you bring the camera?"

"Right here."

"Mom, you sit here. Dr. Anderson, you sit here. Now everyone smile and say 'cheese.'"

Bill Waller stood at the end of the bed and lined us up. The flash went off. "Now don't anybody move until I have a chance to check this. Nope, not good enough. Let me try again. Sherri, Dr. Anderson, why don't you both lean in a little? That's good. Now smile."

The flash went off again. We all relaxed while Bill checked the result. "I like this one. Here let me show you."

Even with the small screen on the camera you could see it was a good photo. It was good because right in the center was the biggest smile I had ever seen.

As I got up to go April took my hand. "Dr. Anderson, you were right," she said. "Miracles do occur. This has been the best Christmas ever." April gave my hand a squeeze.

The Sheriff drove me home. He rattled on about names from the past. I made appropriate comments as we went. My mind was on something else. My mind was on being a doctor for one last time, on caring for a patient, on caring for somebody. It made all the difference.

When the Sheriff left me at the front steps I noted Marge's car parked on the side of the house. "Marge, where are you?" I yelled as I entered the house.

I heard an answer coming from the laundry room. Marge had collected all the dirty towels and linen from the barn. She was busy trying to scrub them clean.

"Marge, what are you doing here?"

"Well, this pile here I think I can get clean, but that pile over there is too far gone. I could try if you want me to."

"Don't worry about it. Just throw them all out. I thought I was losing them all when I took them to the barn last night. Now, what are you doing here?"

Marge's shoulders slumped. "I didn't mean to intrude, Doctor. But Mary Johnston called to tell me that there was an ambulance out at the Anderson place. I just thought I would come over to see if there was anything I could do."

"Marge, my name is Ted. Why don't you call me Ted instead of 'Doctor'. Now, why are you here? You are never here for Christmas. You always spend Christmas with one of your children."

Marge went back to scrubbing. I waited for her to find the words. "All three of my children thought I was spending Christmas with one of the others so they made arrangements to visit their in-laws. When they found out they all invited me along, but, I don't know, I just didn't feel right. Oh, it hasn't been too bad. All three visited last week and I spent the morning talking to grandchildren. Jenny is going to bring her children over in a couple of days."

She had stopped scrubbing. I took the bush out her hand. Her eyes were wet. "You don't need to do this," I told her. "Have you eaten yet? You probably haven't eaten. Why don't I make us a couple of sandwiches? I've got some sliced turkey."

Marge started a smile. "Why, I can do that, Doctor."

I put a finger up. "Ted. I said my name is Ted. And no you can't." I put my hands on Marge's shoulders and steered her towards the living room. "You job is to find some Christmas music on the radio." She started hesitantly in that direction. "And turn it up so I can hear it in the kitchen. I'll make the sandwiches on toast with butter. I don't have any mayo, but I do have some tomato and lettuce. How about some clam chowder? I've got some real good clam chowder I can heat up. And some egg nog, I haven't had egg nog in years."

I repaired to the kitchen and got to work. Pretty soon I heard the sounds of Christmas carols coming from the living room. It took me awhile, but eventually I had everything on trays. When I carried them out to Marge she said something complimentary. I turned down the radio so we could talk as we ate. I told her about April and little Theodora. We talked about a lot of things. It turned out her Joe had served in the Pacific. He had waded ashore a couple times. We might even have shared a foxhole together.

Before we knew it the sun was going down. Marge didn't want to drive at night. It seemed wrong to break it up, especially with an empty house. Marge did not want to give the busybody who called her about the ambulance any more ammunition so I walked her out to her car and watched until she pulled onto the road.

I looked up at the sky. It was a darkening blue. Not too much longer and the sun would be totally gone. I hoped the stars would be out. There was something I wanted to do.

I went back inside to bundle up. Then I headed over to the barn to check on the stock. When I had passed out some feed and made sure there was enough water I stood in the doorway of the barn and watched the first stars pop into view. While I was standing there I wondered whether it was time to sell the old place, to move into town where I could see more people. I probably could give my hired hand a good deal. Maybe I could use the proceeds to start a college fund for little Teddy. I looked up again. It was dark with a lot of stars. Perfect.

I headed out to the middle of the field where I had been the night before. I looked up. The night was filled with stars and I was filled with the same sense of awe, of mystery, of wonder that I felt as a young boy looking at these same stars. Not wanting to miss anything I turned and turned until I was dizzy. Tears streamed from my eyes, but I was never happier. Finally, I stopped turning. I took off my hat. Looking at the sky straight above me I yelled to make sure I was heard. "Now I know why."

The Garden

I was in my office at the church trying to write my sermon for the next Sunday. The text I had chosen was one of my favorites, Matthew 7:1-2, "Judge not lest ye be judged. For with what judgment ye judge, ye shall be judged." I used that verse as a subject for a sermon at least once a year. There are so many good verses in the Bible, but that one keeps calling me back. To me it was a simple but profound plea for compassion, for putting yourself on the side of the other person. I probably had not lived up to it. My temper got the best of me sometimes. I can control my temper so that no one else will notice how upset I am, but my wife notices. Still, it is a good rule by which to live. And I do try.

I sat there in front of my computer contemplating one of my favorite Bible verses and nothing came. I copied out the verse. I placed quotations around it. Half an hour later I removed the quotations. I went back and read my old sermons. They were not bad, just not what I was feeling right then. I wanted something big, something inspiring.

I ended up staring out the window. It was early December. When I sat down it had been a beautiful blue-sky day. I have always found something peaceful and inspiring in watching the sky. As the afternoon faded the sky had turned a dreary gray, a good match for my mood. The weather reports called for a wintry mix starting in the late afternoon. I finally gave up. If I left early I should miss the weather. I sent my secretary home and turned off the lights.

I decide to make a round of the church. On the front steps the wind blew cold and wet. I could see the Nativity scene was lit. In the center of the lawn the Christmas tree lights were on. As a gust of wind reminded me to button my coat, I thought, "Thank God for Christmas." All the lights, all the excitement made the season a celebration of the coming winter and brightened an otherwise dreary time. Yes, thank God for Christmas.

That was the point. Usually I felt excited by this time of the year. Christmas was coming. I was like a little kid. I would drive home by different routes so I could see the different Christmas lights. Buying a tree and trimming it were just such lovely rituals. I just loved everything there was about Christmas. This year I just could not feel any excitement. Today was especially bad. I was frustrated by not being able to write a sermon. The weather was bad. I just did not feel at peace and I did not know why. My wife seemed happy. I was unaware of any problems with our kids. Oh, there was the usual stuff, but there was nothing big. I decide to sit in the sanctuary for a while before heading home.

A church is really a second home to me. The only time I feel as much peace is when I hold my wife. I had been at this church for over a decade now. I liked the people even the troublesome ones. The building was old, but there was a simple elegance to it. I could sit in any of the pews and before long I would have lost myself in a feeling of calm and belonging. It was a feeling I tried to pass along to my parishioners.

I sat in the back. The sanctuary was dark the only light coming from a series of spotlights focused on the cross and the stained glass windows. I waited for that feeling of peace to come over me. There was something just at the edge of my consciousness that would not let me relax. After fifteen minutes or so I decided to give it up for the day. It was a day lost, no sermon, no peace. I should have spent the day doing home calls on shut-ins.

I decide to walk up to check on the lights. When I got to the front pew I was surprised to find someone kneeling in prayer. My first reaction was not to disturb him, but I had already made too much noise. He looked up at me. It was one of our senior high students, Tommy Johnson. He had been crying.

"Rev. Stevens," he said as he wiped away the tears.

"Tommy, it's good to see you."

"I was just going," Tommy said as he stood and turned away.

I reached out and grabbed his arm. That was just so unlike me. I am usually passive, too passive at times. Tommy's whole body tensed. He struggled to get away. I grabbed his arm with my other hand.

"Let me go. Please, let me go. I have to get home. I didn't know it was wrong to be here."

That shook me. Where had I gone wrong that a member of my church would think that I would think it wrong for them to be in church? If asked how I would have reacted I would have said that it was time to let the young man go, but I just tightened my grip. Then I said the first thing that came into my mind, "Judge not lest ye be judged."

Tommy stopped struggling. He still would not look at me, but he said, "Those are just words."

"No, Tommy, those words are my life."

I let go of his arm and he turned toward me. In the dim light I thought I could see tears were running down his face. And just for a moment we faced each other; two creatures, barely seen, lit only by the light reflected from the altar.

"It is never wrong to pray in church," I told him. "God is just waiting for you to turn toward Him that He may show you His grace. Why don't the two of us sit down and talk about this? I don't know whether I can be of any help, but I'd like to try."

We sat down in the front pew of the church. Tommy was hunched over almost in a position of prayer, not looking at me, his hands under his legs, his whole body rocking gently. I was on his left. I leaned back with one arm resting over the back of the pew turned towards him. Then we were silent.

The church was so silent you could hear the traffic outside in the rain. The silence seemed to float about us. Suddenly he blurted out, "I got a girl pregnant." He glanced at me then went back to his gentle rocking motion.

I waited. When the silence seemed long enough Tommy went on, "I've been dating the same girl for a couple of years now. A few months ago her parents were out of town. I went over to her place to watch a movie. We were getting something to eat when the idea of having a couple of drinks with alcohol in them came to us. We had one. Then we had another. We didn't want to have any more because we thought her Dad might notice. Then we started to fool around. We've fooled around before but we never went very far. This time one thing led to another and we had sex. It was the first time for both of us. We didn't talk about it then or since. Everything seemed to be normal for the next month or so. Then she stopped calling me on my cell phone. She wouldn't answer my calls to her cell. When I e-mailed her plans for a date she always had something she had to do with her family. Finally, I tracked her down at school. I asked her if she was breaking up with me. She dragged me after her to a spot where no one would hear us then she whispered in my ear, 'I'm pregnant.' I didn't know what to say. She stood there, looked me in the eyes, and said, 'I never want to see or speak to you again.' I just stood there as she walked away. I thought we were in love."

Tommy stopped here. I waited to be sure he was through. "So, I guess we are out of the garden," I told him.

He turned his head so he could look at me. "Aw, what does a garden have to do with it?" Tommy asked.

"I was referring to the Garden of Eden."

Tommy turned away shaking his head. I was obviously a hopeless case. "That's just a story."

"Well, maybe it is and maybe it isn't. I don't want to debate that with you. What I wanted to do was share with you what a teacher of mine once told me. It really is a process for making sense of the world, a way of thinking about what you experience in this world. It has helped me. I think it might help you. But if you don't want to hear it that's okay."

"No, I would like to hear it," Tommy said. Then I watched as he turned toward me, leaned back, crossed his legs, and put an arm over the back of the pew. We were mirror images now.

I started to open my mouth, but I did not know what to say. I had never shared this with anybody, never used it in a sermon, and never used it for counseling. Since that discussion with my teacher I had just used it for my private thoughts. I had always regarded it as a little too different. Now I had someone needing my help. Perhaps it was time that I made myself vulnerable.

"Do you remember Adam and Eve in the Garden?" Tommy nodded. "Good. That was paradise. They were at peace. That paradise, that peace is what we are all after. Do you remember what happens next in the story?"

Tommy didn't hesitate. "They ate an apple," he said.

"That's right. It wasn't just any apple. It was an apple from the tree of knowledge of good and evil. When they had received this new knowledge they were no longer at peace, they no longer belonged in the Garden, and God banished them.

"We work somewhat the same way in our lives. We get comfortable. We have found a way of dealing with our lives. We have made peace with our lives. Then something happens, some new knowledge that shatters that peace and we are knocked out of the garden, again. And it hurts.

"Somewhere in the Bible it is written, 'He who increases knowledge increases sorrow.' I think that is true, but I don't think that it is an excuse to avoid new knowledge. It is just the opposite. When things seem at their worst and we are wandering in the wilderness and in pain it is the choice of turning to Him that brings us closer to God."

I hesitated here. I turned to face the altar and looked to where I knew the cross was. "Sometimes I think that is the answer to why there is evil in the world. Mankind has freedom to make a mess of things, but also has the freedom to turn to God. It is the choice, the act of turning to God that brings us closer to Him."

I bowed my head thinking of what I had just said. It surprised me. I don't think I had ever gotten so philosophical in a counseling session.

"What do you think I should do about my girlfriend?" Tommy asked.

This brought me back out of my meditation. "Well, it is easy to see that she has been knocked out of the Garden. She's in pain trying to deal with something that is tearing apart her life. Her treatment of you probably has nothing to do with you. It is her way of dealing with the situation. You would probably prefer if she came to you so you could handle the situation together, but she is scared. It is safer to reject you than take a chance that you would reject her. So, all you can do is love her. Sometimes that is all anyone can do for another human being. I don't know whether you love her as a spouse, or as a friend, or as a fellow human, but love her. That is presuming you still lover her?"

"I do love her," Tommy said. "But it really hurt to have her tell me she never wanted to see me again."

"Well, now that you know what the problem is you should forgive her. Perhaps you can get the message through that you still love her despite her rejection, despite or because of the pregnancy. Knowing that one person loves you and is there for you is a lot."

"What about my parents?" Tommy asked. "Should I tell them? They'll never understand. They're going to hate me when I tell them."

"Hate is a little strong don't you think?" I said. "They aren't going to be happy with you, but we are never happy with the messenger who brings us new knowledge that kicks us out of the Garden. Remember, what you told them put them in pain and they are trying to deal with it. No matter what they do or say they will never stop loving you. Now as to telling them, I think you must, but you might want to wait until you are sure that your girlfriend has told her parents. Your parents probably can guess who it is that is pregnant and they might call her parents and create a problem."

We were silent again. I would never let the silence lengthen like this in a counseling session. Here in church it seemed right. We were just two humans alone with their God at the same time we shared the experience.

It was Tommy who broke the silence. "I've got to go," he said. He jumped up as if sitting on a spring and started down the pew.

"Wait, Tommy. I'll give you a ride," I told him starting to stand up.

"No, thanks, it's not far," Tommy answered without looking back.

"But the weather?"

Tommy was already a shadow as he moved up the aisle. "I don't mind the weather," he said. "It makes the walk more interesting."

I listened to Tommy's footsteps as he headed out of the sanctuary. It was so quiet I could hear the door to the sanctuary open.

"Mr. Stevens?" I heard Tommy's voice come out of the darkness. I turned, but could not make Tommy out.

"Yes, Tommy."

"Thank you," he said.

"You're welcome, Tommy."

I heard the door to the sanctuary shut. Seconds later I heard the front door crash closed. I was alone.

I have actually contemplated that very idea. Can you ever be alone in church? Are you ever alone anywhere? I felt alone at that moment. Despite his 'thank you' I felt sure I had failed Tommy. Had I spoken to him out of compassion or out of my frustrations with the day? I am a trained, professional counselor, but sometimes I feel I hide behind my professional technique. Perhaps today I should have done just that.

With questions buzzing around my brain I folded my hands and rested them on the rail in front of me. I rested my forehead on my hands. I tried to banish the questions by concentrating on my breath, in and out. I wasn't very successful. I wound up wondering how I ended up feeling this way at Christmas time. Slowly the words 'Christmas time' became synchronized with my breath, 'Christmas' in and 'time' out. That calmed me, stopped the questions whirring around my head.

I looked up. In the dim light I could make out the cross. A thought just filled my whole being. There is a new beginning; there is a new life. I was filled with a feeling of joy so intense I started to cry.

I ran out of the sanctuary and out of the church. After locking the front door I turned and saw the Nativity scene and Christmas tree all lit up. Once again I thought, "There is a new beginning; there is a new life. Thank God for Christmas."

As I ran to my car through the freezing rain I was already plotting the route home that would show me the most spectacular Christmas lights.

Nearly Christmas

It was nearly Christmas many years ago.

I glanced at my watch. Eleven o'clock, in one hour it would be Christmas. In two hours I would be able to head home. I hated to work on Christmas Eve. I had worked every Christmas Eve since the third year in medical school. At first I thought working Christmas Eve was just the price I had to pay for becoming a doctor. Now, with a wife and two children at home I resented missing a time with them that would never come again. Still, moonlighting in the emergency room Christmas Eve paid the bills for Christmas.

There were several good things about working in the emergency room on Christmas Eve. One was that I had Christmas free. The second was the festive mood. The nurses lightened the load by making a party of the night. There were plenty of cookies and cakes. Between the sugar and the coffee I was not going to fall asleep for hours. The third was that it was always a light night. Instead of having twenty patients waiting there were four or five. There was not the time pressure of the usual night. The last was that I might get to go home early. Last year the full-timer sent me home almost an hour early. It was not much, but I was grateful.

I still had patients to see. I went back to work. I reviewed the x-rays on a fractured big toe and set the patient up with some crutches and pain meds. Then I wrote prescriptions for an acute sinus infection. I was drilling a fingernail to relieve the pain caused by a hemorrhage beneath the nail when flashing lights appeared at the ambulance entrance, never a good sign. I hesitated. The last thing I needed was to get involved in a disaster this late in the night. I did not have to worry. Bob, the full-timer, was moving to check it out.

It was a full out disaster. The emergency medical techs wheeled the stretcher into the crash area. The crash cart was opened. Nurses and technicians crowded around. And I went back to work.

I think the next one was a G.I. flu. I ordered some intravenous hydration and a shot to relieve the nausea. I was finishing up with a corneal abrasion, the classic Christmas tree branch in the eye, when Bob approached.

"Carter, could you take a look in this little girls eyes. I've tried to look in, but I can't seem to see anything?" he said. Bob handed me the ophthalmoscope. I went over to take a look.

She was a cute little blonde about three or four years old. I tried to concentrate on the eyes, but the head trauma was obvious. Her pupils were dilated. I flashed the light on high power from one eye to the other hoping for a flicker of movement. There was no response. I bent over to look in the eyes. Blood, there was nothing but blood.

I turned to Bob and told him, "You saw everything there is to see. Both eyes are filled with blood. Not a good prognostic sign when associated with head trauma."

"I'm going to stay here and work on this little girl some more. Why don't you check on her mother," Bob said. Then he handed me the mother's chart and turned away.

I was appalled at what he was asking me to do. I should have refused. Instead I just stood there in shock.

At last, I looked at the chart. The little girl's mother was in one of the back rooms so she was probably not injured. While I headed back there I checked the rest of the chart. The vital signs were normal. My eyes always went to the birth date. We were born in the same year. The fact that we were both thirty-one seemed to make the situation worse. I hesitated at the door thinking that this poor woman needed someone better than me.

I opened the door. The room was dark. Something was wrong. I felt for the light switch. When the light came on I saw a woman passed out on the stretcher. I hit the call button. I yelled that the patient was passed out and I needed a nurse right away.

She woke up then. She had heard me yelling for a nurse. Sitting up she said, "No doctor, really, I'm okay."

I hit the button again and cancelled the call. I introduced myself and started in on the history. Any pain? Any blurred vision? Any double vision? A bloody nose? Any neck pain? And on and on. Then I proceeded with the physical. I listened here and there. I poked and prodded and percussed. I checked strength and sensation. Her reflexes were fine. I checked her eye movements and pupils. Then I looked in her eyes. She was right. She was okay.

I stopped. She took the moment to ask the question I had been dreading. "Doctor, what about my daughter?"

"They were still working on her when I came in here, but they had asked me to look in her eyes. It is something I know about. I am sorry. She is just not going to make it. She was such a cute little girl."

I expected tears, a wail of pain, perhaps a scream of anguish. Instead she asked, "Doctor, do you know anything about dreams?"

"Not very much," I told her.

"Would you mind listening to my dream?" she asked.

"No, not at all," I said.

I sat down on a stool. She was sitting on the edge of the stretcher. Her eyes never left the floor while she was telling her story.

"My daughter and I were driving home from Grandma's house. My husband is flying back from Europe and doesn't get in until Christmas morning. I had stopped at a red light. When the light turned green I started across the intersection. I never saw anything before we were hit. The noise was awful. Then I was ripped in all directions. The car tumbled and somehow ended up on its side. I wasn't knocked out, but it took me a little while to realize where I was. I was strapped in. I couldn't move very well. I checked hands and feet. Everything worked and felt normal. Then I noticed the silence. My daughter should have been crying and yelling for me. There was just silence. I tried to twist around so I could see her. I couldn't do it. I could see her door caved in. Then I cried. I didn't want to cry, but the tears just poured out of me. Through a corner of the windshield I could see a star. For some reason seeing the star comforted me.

"It wasn't long before the silence was broken by sirens. The rest passed in a blur. The ambulance people and the firemen got us out of the car. I saw one ambulance take my daughter away. I was loaded into another ambulance. I answered a lot of questions. They even put a collar on me.

"I was wheeled in here. A nurse came. She asked more questions, took my blood pressure and temperature. I asked her what was going on. She said she did not know and left.

"I was alone. I've never felt that alone. I was angry at you people for leaving me alone. I tried to close my eyes, to shut everything out. The light was too bright. I took off the collar, got up and turned off the light. When I laid back on the stretcher, staring up at the dark ceiling, I thought I could see that same star, the one I saw from my wrecked car.

"The next thing I knew everything went dark. It was as if I was surrounded by an impenetrable fog. I was scared. Then a star appeared, faintly at first, but slowly it grew brighter.

"A voice called out from the dark. 'Woman,' it said, 'I need your help.'"

"A man appeared out of the dark. 'My wife, he said, 'is having a child. Will you help us?'"

"I told him a simple, 'Yes.'" He led away. I followed. And the star shone brighter.

"It was not long before we came to a rough shelter. A fire was burning. A woman lay on a blanket spread over straw. She was in pain. I went to her and comforted her.

"The man said, 'This is my wife Mary and I am Joseph.'

"Mary was in labor. I had never heard or read about the pain before. I didn't know whether it was a difficult labor, but it was labor. The labor went on for some time. The pain became worse. The baby was about to be born. I delivered the baby and wrapped in a cloth. I held him for just a second before handing him to Mary. After all that pain it was a glorious moment. I kneeled there beside Mary and the infant Jesus with Joseph looking on and I was totally at peace. Then you came in and woke me up.

"So, Doctor, what do you think my dream means?"

I was stunned. I sat there without a clue. The silence lengthened. Finally, for the first time since she started her tale she looked at me and said, "I think I'm pregnant."

I jumped off the stool. "That's good news," I said. "It is good news? Isn't it? I mean I hope it is good news."

"Yes, it is good news," she said. "My husband and I have been trying for over a year. I haven't tested it yet, but I am late, almost a month late, and I am never late. My husband doesn't even know."

"We ought to do a test," I said. "We need to find out if the baby is alright."

"No, please, Doctor, I feel fine. I'll get tested later this week, but not today. I just wanted you to know because you've been so kind."

I nodded my assent. Again, the silence grew. I looked at my watch. The time was almost one-thirty.

"I have to go now," I told her. "My wife will be wondering where I am. Is there something else I can do for you?"

"No, thank you, Doctor."

"I'll send a nurse in."

With that I stepped through the door and closed it. I ran down the corridor until I found a nurse. I dragged her to the room and waited until she entered.

I had left other patients waiting too long. I rushed to the nursing station and searched for my charts. Jerry had taken over for Bob. He saw me across the emergency room and started my way. "What are you doing here?" he asked. "The nurses told me you had left. I've already taken care of all your patients. It's Christmas. Go home."

I wished him a Merry Christmas, collected my stuff, and headed for the parking lot. It had just stopped snowing. My car was covered with snow. I was in the midst of clearing it when a thought struck. It had been snowing when that lady had been in her accident. How had she seen a star? I looked up. Past the parking lot lights the clouds were just breaking up. One star was visible. And I wondered, "Was that the one?"

Perfect

Everything was perfect.

I loved to enter my office by the front door. There was a side door so doctors did not run into their patients in the waiting area, but it took me over twenty years to build this office so I enjoyed the full experience. When you first entered there was the huge waiting area with the immaculate furniture. There was a place for children to play. The furniture was arranged so people could have privacy. It was all laid out scientifically. On the other side was the business office. I never got tired of hearing the phones ring, of seeing people scurrying around getting the practice's paperwork done.

When I had passed through the waiting area I was in the doctor's work area. There was a long corridor with exam rooms, treatment, rooms and more waiting rooms. All the rooms had lights on the outside to tell the doctors and nurses where they had to go. Finally, I reached my office. This is where I do my paperwork and see patients for consultations. I had a special desk made just for me. The top is this cherry wood with a grain so beautiful that I keep the top as clean as possible. I am an oncologist so I will see people for problems such as cancer and lymphoma. After I examine them I will bring them into the office. I will sit behind the desk. They will sit on the other side. Usually they will have someone with them. It is sort of interesting to see. Often the significant other is in more pain from the situation than the patient. The desk is so big it can hold everything I need. It holds diagrams and models and charts and statistics and treatment plans on every sort of tumor so the patient can feel informed and make good decisions.

There is so much that I can do for patients now. I have nurses that specialize in intravenous therapy every bit as good as the nurses I knew from my fellowship days at the University. I have a nurse that specialized in all the experimental protocols my partners and I were involved in with the University. I have a pain nurse that I had trained myself that is super in dealing with pain management problems. I have a nurse I trained to answer most of the phone questions the group gets so the doctors do not have to be tied up on the phone. And, if that time comes, I can turn the patients over to an excellent hospice program that I helped develop.

I have three partners now. They all joined me in the last six years. I spent the first fourteen years by myself wondering whether my predictions of growth would ever come true. Now, almost twenty-one years after I started a practice here, my dream was coming true. Yes, everything was perfect. That is until he showed up.

I remember it pretty clearly. I reviewed his chart before entering the exam room. His surgeon was Tom Miller. He had a bad tumor that would probably kill him in six months. He did not have insurance. He was the manager of a convenience store that did not offer insurance. I did not relish this exam. I was not going to be able to do much for him. Oh, there was some experimental stuff we could try that might give him an extra six months or a year, but a cure was impossible. Bad tumor. Bad humor. I closed the chart, took a couple of seconds to collect myself, and opened the door.

What I saw was not what I was expecting. He was sitting on the exam table when I stepped into the room. I went into my normal introduction. He hopped of the table and held out his hand. He said, "I'm Jim. It's a pleasure to meet you."

I took his hand and returned his greeting. Jim appeared to be in his mid-thirties. He was tall, seemingly taller than the six feet two on the chart. He was thin, but not that thinness I see in patients when their tumor or the treatment has starved them. He had light brown hair that he wore on the long side with a short beard that was neat. He smiled as if it really was a pleasure to meet me. He had light brown eyes that held mine. I have met other individuals that try to hold your eyes. They usually come off as aggressive. Jim gave you this feeling of searching concern. I half expected him to ask whether I was having a good day.

I am usually all business, trying to save precious seconds, trying not to hold up other patients. If a patient offers a hand we shake and move on. With Jim it was different. I was struck by something that I don't usually see in my practice. Jim was fearless.

At last I asked Jim to get back on the exam table. The exam proceeded with the usual questions and instructions. When I finished I told him that he could get dressed and that he should wait there until a nurse came for him. When I closed the door I ran off to take care of another patient.

The next time I saw Jim he was sitting in one of the patient chairs in my office. He was alone, no significant other. He stood as I entered. I waived him back to his seat. Passing the desk I busied myself with the scans, placing the important views on the x-ray box. Then I sat down to take one more look at the path report, the lab tests, and Dr. Miller's letter.

I was about to start my discussion of his tumor and what we could do about it when I thought, "Maybe he doesn't know he could have someone in here."

"Before we start is there someone you would like to hear this with you? You don't have to go through this alone, you know," I told him.

Jim's smile never wavered. "I am never alone," he said. "Besides, you're here."

I started in on my discussion. Over the years I have gotten pretty good at this. I think I know just how far to go in laying out all the facts without getting too depressing or sugar coating something that shouldn't be sugar coated. I think I know when to stop for interruptions, how to give people a little space. Jim never asked any questions so I went right through to the treatment options. For Jim they weren't good. Some patients were getting a year or even two more than expected with something new. Given an extra year there might be another breakthrough. There's always hope.

"How sick will the treatment make me?" Jim asked.

"To be honest, pretty sick," I told him. "You have to remember that without treatment your tumor will make you pretty sick."

"I don't know, Dr. Ross. It is something I'm going to have to think about," he said.

"That's okay," I responded. "Take your time, talk it over with someone, and get back to me in a few days."

"I'm afraid it will be a lot longer than that. I want to take a trip," he told me.

"A trip? Well, that sounds like a good idea. How long will it be? A week? Two?" I asked.

"I was thinking of a couple of months. You see, I've never been more than about twenty miles from my home. I'd like to get out and see some of the country. Maybe when I get back I'll be ready."

Two months? He could be dead in two months. I thought about lecturing him, but there was just something about him that stopped me. While I was thinking he had stood up and offered his hand over the desk. I stood up and took his hand. He held my hand between the two of his and said, "I want to thank you for seeing me."

He dropped my hand and turned toward the door. "You will think about this?" I asked.

Jim stopped at the door. Turning to look at me he said, "Yes, Doctor, I will think about it and I promise to come in and tell you what I've decided."

With that the door closed behind him. I sat down heavily in my chair. At that moment I felt a failure. Oh, it wasn't that Jim could not commit to treatment right then and there. I even encourage patients to go home and think about it. I did not know why I felt that way. That made it harder.

After stewing for a while I scribbled 'no charge' on the billing form. I walked the chart out to the front desk and told our receptionist, "Sue, that last patient, the one who just left, there's to be no charge." Just saying 'no charge' made me feel better about the whole thing.

Sue held up some cash. "But, Dr. Ross, he's already paid," she told me. "He just dropped $250 on the desk. He said, 'I think this will cover it.' Before I could say anything he smiled, said, 'Thank you,' and was gone."

I stared after the door as if that would bring me an answer. Sue finally asked, "What do you want me to do? Should I deposit it and issue a refund?"

I would be damned if I took his money. If the office sent him a check Jim would never cash it. "Give it to charity," I told her. I pivoted and went back to work.

My wife Annie asked me to pick up a few things at the market on the way home from work. With the kids in college she was back to working part-time at the hospital. She would not get home until after me and it would be even later if she had to make a stop. I was cruising around the store when I ran into a familiar face. This has gotten to be a frequent occurrence, but this face I could not quite place. She looked at me and said, "Hello, Doctor." I smiled and said, "Hello."

We went our separate ways. I knew I had seen her as a patient. I had not taken care of her, though. I would have remembered her. Sometimes I see people as the significant other or as the driver for mom or dad. I was pretty sure I had seen her as a patient. I even thought I could remember what her problem was. Perhaps she was seeing one of my partners.

We ran into each other again at the produce section. She took a quick look at me and then busied herself with the apples. I did not feel I could ignore her so I said, "I hope everything is going well."

Again she gave me that quick look up and back to the apples. "Yes, everything is fine," she said.

Ever curious I could not resist asking, "Who's taking care of you now?"

Again that quick look up and then back to finding the apples she wanted. "Dr. Papadapoulos."

I had expected her to name one of my partners. Dr. Papadapoulos was the doctor who recruited me. He must be 75 now. He was a sweetheart, though. "Dr. Papadapoulos. You're in good hands. He's the best," I told her.

Then a thought struck me. Dr.Papadapoulos' office was twenty miles away in the next town. I was not even sure he kept up his hospital privileges at our hospital. Why would someone go to all that trouble? What had my office done to make her do that? It is not often you get a chance to do a little research on your own office. I had to barge ahead and say, "I hope you don't mind me asking, but why did you go all the way over to Dr. Papadapoulos? Was there something my office did that was wrong?"

This time she answered without looking up. I could not hear her so I said, "I'm sorry, but I couldn't make that out."

She looked me in the eyes this time and did not look away until she was finished saying, "I said that I was looking for some compassion."

I was thunderstruck. I had expected some problem with getting appointments, or insurance, or a bill. Perhaps she had gotten into an argument with the receptionist. What she had said was so far away from anything I was thinking that I was speechless. She had already moved away before I could call out a weak, "Thank you."

On the drive home the thought of Dr. Papadapoulos started me thinking back to how I had come to this town. Annie and I had met during my residency. She was a nurse at the University Hospital where I had trained. We had gotten married during my last year of residency. By the end of my fellowship she was about to deliver our first, Jeff, Jr. I wanted to stay and join the team at the University. They had offered me a position. I presumed that was where I would end up, but Annie was not feeling that way.She wanted to return to her hometown. Especially with a child on the way she did not want to raise a child in the city or even in the suburbs. Now I was a child of the suburbs so I did not see anything wrong with raising children in the suburbs. As you might guess, this led to some discussions. It was finally agreed that I would at least look at the situation.

That is where Dr. Papadapoulos came in. He had an oncology practice covering two hospitals of similar size about twenty miles apart. He was getting tired of traveling between the two hospitals so he wanted to bring in someone to take over at the hospital in Annie's hometown.

I remember the first time I went to his office. I think his waiting room was about six by six with only four chairs and magazines from five years before. His wife was his only employee. My heart sunk. This was not the way I envisioned practicing medicine. But Annie really wanted this so I took a look around.

What I saw was a new interstate passing next to town. There was new construction of homes. Some of the farms in the area were being bought up and developed. The hospital was building a new medical office building and down next to the interstate sat a new office building with another just breaking ground. The town looked like it was ripe for growth with families looking for a little larger home moving out here where they could afford it. I decided to give it a shot.

I cannot say it has been easy, but things worked out. The major difference was living in a small town. In the suburbs you were anonymous. Here you end up going to the same restaurant for lunch everyday. You get 'honey'd' and 'dear'd.' Pretty soon you find out you and the waitress have kids in school together. Or you go to the same church. Or you have taken care of a relative. Pretty soon you are not waited on by a stranger, you are waited on by a friend, and you are 'Doc' and they are Joan or Sally or whatever. Same sort of thing happens in the neighborhood. Instead of always looking for the bigger house you sort of burrow in. It is a real solid feel to life.

Sundays are different, too. By the time I had gotten through with college and medical school I had stopped going to church. I was a little too intellectual for all that. Annie wanted to go to church so I went. I liked it, too. I am probably not much of a Christian, but it feels good seeing the same people week after week. Some live on the same block or just the next street over. When you have worked on a church bazaar or a bake sale with people you begin to think of them differently. Again, it gives life a real solid feel.

So, if everything has worked out and life is good why was I awake at 2 am staring at the ceiling. I was wide awake. Annie lay next to me sound asleep. If I put my arms around her I knew I would relax and fall asleep, but I did not want to wake her. Maybe if I tried to imagine the stars on the ceiling I would relax.

At one time I could picture the stars with ease. When I was a kid I was fascinated by the heavens at night. I had my own telescope and spent hours watching the stars. My favorite thing was going to a planetarium. I even wanted to be an astronaut. Then in high school I sprouted to six feet four. Someone dashed my hopes by telling me that you could not be an astronaut at six four. I never checked. I should have checked. Then I turned to astronomy in college. Sophomore year my mother's younger sister died of cancer. I set off to become a cancer specialist. I think that is the last time I looked up at the stars. I've had my nose to the grindstone ever since.

Orion was easy to visualize though I forgot how the lesser stars looked. I was just trying to remember the relationship between the big and small dipper and the north star when Annie turned over. She laid a hand on my shoulder. "Why are you awake? Did something happen at work today?"

"No, nothing happened at work," I told her.

"Are you not feeling well?"

"No, I feel fine."

We were quiet for a while. Annie rolled onto her side and draped her arm over my chest. "What is it?" she asked.

I thought for a minute trying to figure out exactly how to put it. I just went ahead and told her what was on my mind. "Am I compassionate?"

"Compassionate! Is that what has you up in the middle of the night?"

"Well, it's something someone said to me today."

"Jeff, you are a great doctor, but you are a perfectionist. I've seen how it eats you up when something you did not expect happens to one of your patients. You look after every detail. There's something that you never have been able to deal with as a doctor that I leaned as a nurse. People live, people get sick, and people die. There is only so much you can do and you are doing everything you can. If you have to do anything more it will kill you. Now hold me so I can fall asleep. It's freezing."

With that she rolled away from me onto her side. I slid over and draped an arm around her. I kissed the back of her head and thought, "Smart woman."

Two months went by and I had not given Jim another thought. One afternoon I picked up a chart before entering an exam room. There he was. I smiled at the thought of seeing him again. There was just something about him. As I opened the door to the exam room I remember wondering what he would look like and hoping he was not in too much pain.

Jim stood up and took my hand as soon as I offered it. "Dr. Ross, it is good to see you again," he said.

"Jim, it is good to see you, too. Why don't you hop back up on the table and let me do a little exam?"

"I really didn't come for an exam, Doctor. I just wanted to talk."

"Please, let me do my job."

Jim nodded and lay down on the table. I went through the exam. Blood pressure and pulse were good. Weight was down only three pounds from the last visit. Not bad. The conjunctiva and mucous membranes showed good color so he was probably not anemic, yet. Lungs were clear. Heart tones were strong and regular. He did not show any sign of weakness in his extremities and there was no loss of sensation. The only problem was the abdomen. There was a slight sense of tenderness and perhaps a mass that I had not felt before. The liver also felt slightly enlarged and, I thought, tender, though Jim tried to hide it. As I went through the physical I peppered him with question. Everything was answered with "Fine," or "No problem."

When I had finished I told him, "Jim, why don't you get dressed and go over to my office and we'll have that talk."

I took the chart with me and went to tend to a couple of patients before entering my office. When I did open the door Jim started to rise. I waved him back to his seat and took my position behind the desk. I went over everything again. When I was satisfied I asked Jim, "So, have you made up your mind about the chemo? I can't promise much, but I am willing to try."

There was still that sense of being in a presence that I did not understand. Jim shook his head, "No, Doctor, I do not want the chemo. I am dying. It won't be long now, three, four weeks. I really came to tell you about my trip and a decision I have made."

I started to say something, but Jim held up his hand to stop me. "I wanted to tell you about my trip," he said.

I nodded and he continued, "I drove through the Rockies. It was amazing, ten, twelve feet of snow. I had always wanted to go out to the mountains during winter and see all that snow. Got stuck in a blizzard. I suppose I should have been scared, but that doesn't make any sense any more. I got out of the truck. In a few steps I could not make out the truck except for its lights. The wind was whipping the snow along and it was coming down so heavy I was in a world of white. Couldn't drive any place so I just waited it out in the truck. The nicest people came by the next morning and dug me out. Had a cup of coffee for me, too.

"I went to the top of a mountain on one of those ski lifts. Had to take a ski lesson just to get on. Looking out over that world of white with the clouds drifting around the mountains, the blue sky between the clouds. I don't think I can describe it, but it filled me with such a sense of wonder. Made it down the mountain on those rented skis. Couldn't have fallen more than a dozen times.

"Anyway, I wandered here and there and ended up down by the Mexican border in the desert. I found a little town there and stayed about a week. Every night I would drive out in the desert until I couldn't see the lights of the town. Then I parked by the side of the road and turned out all the lights. I lay down in the bed of my truck and looked up at the stars. It was unbelievable. I had never seen so many stars. I could see the Milky Way. Have you ever looked up at the stars and wondered? There was this sense of awe as I looked at them, a sense that was humbling, but there was something else, something calming. I went out there night after night trying to figure out things out, all alone. It was about the fifth or sixth night I was out there that I realized what was making me feel so good. It was the sense that I was part of all that, always have been, always will be. Then an idea came to me, something I wanted to get done before I die."

He had been pacing around the room as he talked fiddling with this or that. With this last sentence he stopped and looked directly at me. The change that came about him was quite sudden and startled me with his intensity. I was just about to say something when he took a couple of steps to the front of the desk, grabbed my hand to shake it, said, "Thank you, Doctor," and was gone.

He had left so suddenly I was stunned. Then I remembered what happened with the last bill and raced to the front desk. Sue was already heading my way. She had some dollar bills in her hand. "Dr. Ross, that Jim person already paid. I told him you didn't want his money, but he just laid it on the desk and said, 'Then give it to charity.' What do you want me to do?"

I looked down the corridor as if Jim was still there. I had the feeling that I had not seen the last of Jim. I gave Sue Jim's chart.

Turning back to the exam rooms I said, "Well, you heard the man. Give it to charity."

As I strode down the corridor Sue called after me, "He seems awfully nice. Is he going to be alright?"

I stopped and turned. I took a couple of steps back so I could say it quietly. "I wouldn't worry about Jim," I told her. "I think everything is alright for Jim." Then I headed off for my next patient.

I think it was three weeks later, Monday of Easter week. The kids, Jeff and Allie, were home from college. Annie always wanted to do something as a family, but all the kids wanted to do was borrow a car so that they could go out with their friends. I was in my office finishing some paperwork before leaving for the day when one our nurses, Cynthia, came into my office. She stood in front of the desk while I finished dictating. When I had finished I asked, "What's up?"

"We got this message from someone called Jim," she said. "He asked if you could stop by his house tonight after work."

Hearing Jim's name again was like a cold knife in the gut. I just knew this couldn't be good. "So what did you tell him?" I asked.

"We tried to tell him that you did not make house calls and we tried to set him up with an appointment, but he said he was too sick to come to the office. We suggested calling the rescue squad, but he told us not to do that. He was very insistent in a nice way and he felt sure you would make an exception. He left these directions."

I took the slip of paper that Cynthia handed to me. Jim's house was on the same side of town as mine. It was about five miles further out off one of the main roads. At least it would not take all night getting there and back. I looked up at Cynthia. "I'll take care of this. You ought to head home," I told her.

When Cynthia left I started a search for my old black bag. I found it in the bottom of a closet, had to dust it off. I had not used the bag in years. Now the question became what to put into it. I put my stethoscope in as well as a portable blood pressure cuff. I added a few syringes and alcohol swabs. At the medicine cabinet I put in a couple of vials for nausea and signed out some narcotics. I was heading out the door when I remembered to put a prescription pad in the bag.

The trip out to Jim's place was not bad, though I drove past his house once. On the way back I stopped at his drive and checked the number on his mailbox. They matched the ones I had been given so I pulled into the drive. The house had a light on, but not much else. I sat there thinking about my next move for awhile. The only thing to do was get out of my car and head for the house. If it was the wrong house maybe whoever lived here could point me in right direction.

I got out of my car, took a few steps toward the house, and looked up. There was a gap in the trees and I could see Orion. The stars looked brighter here a few miles outside of town. I was appreciating the view when a voice said, "You must be the doctor."

I must have jumped five feet. When I collected myself and turned toward the voice I found a middle age man who said, "I am sorry to have startled you. I'm Rev. Thompson. I have that church you passed at the turn off."

His hand was out so I took it. "I'm Dr. Ross," I said.

"Jim told me he was expecting a doctor. Why don't I show you the way," he said.

Rev. Thompson turned and led me up the walkway. I often end up meeting my patient's pastor so I was a little surprised that I had never run into Rev. Thompson. "So, you're Jim's Pastor?" I asked him.

"I wish," he answered. "I've been trying to get Jim to come to my church since I moved here four years ago. No, I know Jim from that convenience store he runs. One of the first days I was here I stopped in there for a cup of coffee and we got to talking. I ended up spending over three hours there. All that time people are coming and going. He knows them all by name. He's got a good word for everybody and he's introducing me to everybody. He tells them where the church is. He even knows when the service is. He doesn't even charge for the cup of coffee. I figure he must be part of the congregation, but I had not seen him in church.

"I end up going back there for a cup of coffee once or twice a week. In a couple of months I'm going there everyday except Sunday. Jim is still introducing me to new people. One day when there aren't any other people around I ask him why I've never seen him in church. I expect him to tell me that he belongs to one of those big churches downtown. Instead he takes me outside. It was about 7:00 am on a crystal clear day. He told me to close my eyes. Then he asked to breathe in deeply. It had rained the night before. There was a freshness in the air. You could smell the Earth, the wet soil, the trees. Then he said, "Listen." The birds were singing to each other. In the distance there was a train and the whine of an eighteen-wheeler heading downhill. Then he walks me over to the edge of a field and tells me to look. It was late spring and the corn was coming up, row upon row. Birds were swooping here and there. Finally, he tells me to look up at the sky and take a few deep breaths. There was an isolated cloud, just a wisp really against a blue, blue sky, but there was something lovely in its loneliness. Then Jim looked me in the eye and said, 'This is my church.'"

"I never brought it up again. Jim and I are just friends, but there isn't a day goes by that he doesn't teach me something."

We were standing at the front door. Rev. Thompson opened the door and stepped through. I followed him into the house. "Jim," he yelled out, " it's Bill. I've got the doctor with me."

A voice I recognized as Jim's called out from somewhere in the back, "Thanks, Bill. Just send him on back."

Bill pointed down the hallway. "Jim's down there and to the left," he said. Then he called out, "I'm leaving again, Jim. I'll see you tomorrow."

I watched Bill disappear through the front door. When he had left I headed down a short hallway to where light was coming from a room.

I was not really prepared for what I saw. Jim lay on the bed in some loose fitting clothes. I got the feeling that all his clothes fit loose now. He was propped up by some pillows. There was a reading light on next to the table and a book was open on the bed.

"Hi, Dr. Ross. You'll have to forgive me if I don't get up. I barely make it to the bathroom on my hands and knees. I'm not sure I'll be able to do even that much longer."

"Hi, Jim," I said. "You're not looking too good."

"I'm not feeling too good," he said.

"Look, what do you want me to do?" I asked him.

"Did I ever tell you that my father was a carpenter?" he asked. "He built this place. When we put on the addition I helped. I was a carpenter for a number of years until my father died. Then I found building a house to be lonesome work so I started in the convenience store. Meet more people that way. My father and I built all the furniture in the house. The furniture really is something special. My father carved all the pieces. I always thought he was something of an artist. Mom got into it. All the furniture covering is homemade."

Jim paused here. I think that short discourse took all the energy he could muster. I stepped up to the bed. "Jim, what do you want me to do for you?" I asked.

Jim's eyes locked with mine. It was that look I remembered from our first encounter. He was all there for you, searching for what made you ache inside. He held this just long enough. When the moment had stretched to the point when it might have felt strange his focus changed. I followed his gaze to the bag I held in my left arm.

"Did you plan on easing my pain?" Jim asked.

I felt very uncomfortable. What was I doing there with the drugs in the bag? "Is that what you want?" I responded.

Jim smiled. "You know what I would like?" he said. "How about a glass of water? Why don't you go out to the kitchen and get us both a glass of water? While you're out there have a look around."

I went out to the kitchen. I opened the door to the refrigerator that gave me enough light to see the light switch. Switching on the light was a treat. All the cabinets were handmade. On each was a carved a different scene of animals and trees and mountains. The cabinet handles were all carved in the shapes of different animals. The small table on which I placed the bag was carved, as were the chairs. Everywhere I looked there were depictions of nature carved in wood, stitched on the curtains, painted on the walls.

I searched through the cabinets until I found some glasses. The refrigerator held a bottle of water so I filled the glasses with cold water. I carried the two glasses into the bedroom leaving the black bag behind.

Jim took the glass and sipped off a fraction before placing it on the nightstand. I was not sure what to do with the glass I held until I realized I was thirsty. I drained about half of it. I could not find another place to put it so I placed it on the nightstand, too.

"I see you left your black bag behind," Jim said.

"Seriously, Jim, what am I doing here? If you are having pain I can give you a shot or write a prescription for something. If its nausea there are medicines I can give you. I can get some hospice nurses in here. They could give you a hand. We could even admit you to the hospital. Maybe you have longer to live than you think. What is it you want?"

For the first time since I had arrived Jim looked away. I thought I saw something dark pass over his features, a sign of the effort it took to hold a simple conversation. It passed and Jim turned back with a smile.

"You're right, Doc. I am in pain and I am nauseous, but I prefer to control it without drugs. As to hospice, it might not seem like it right now, but I am surrounded by friends. Right after you leave a couple are delivering some milkshakes. I wasn't sure what flavor I wanted. I think I've decided on chocolate."

"That's wonderful," I told him, "but where do I fit in all this?"

"You know what I really miss?" he asked. "Meeting new people, hearing their stories. What I would really like is if you would pull up that chair over there and tell me about yourself."

I pulled the chair next to the bed and sat down. I was wondering where to start when Jim said. "Why don't you tell me about your hometown, the house and neighborhood you grew up in?"

I started off. Jim was a good listener. A nod here, a question there whenever I slowed down kept me going. At one point he closed his eyes. I stopped talking. I thought he had fallen asleep. "Don't stop," Jim told me, "I am just trying to visualize what you were telling me." So, I went on.

I had just talked about my high school when Jim put up a hand. "Time for you to go home to Annie, Dr. Ross. She'll be worried about you."

I took my leave and started for the door. I was feeling a bit guilty about leaving Jim alone. I was stepping through the door when Jim said, "Don't worry Dr. Ross, I'll be all right. What I would like is if you could come tomorrow about the same time."

"I'll try," I told him.

I headed for the front door. Before I reached it an older couple came in carrying bags from an ice cream store. "We're Ethel and Bob," the woman told me. "How's Jim doing?"

"He's doing about as well as could be expected," I told her.

"Good," she said going past me. "Jim, its Ethel and Bob. We've got milkshakes."

"Bring them on in here," I heard Jim say.

I watched Ethel and Bob disappear down the hallway. I headed for my car. It was not until I started my car that I realized how late it was. I must have talked for over two hours. I left a message with Annie that I would be a little late. I had expected to spend fifteen to twenty minutes with Jim. It had turned into two and a half hours. I grabbed my cell phone. It was off. I turned it on. There were a couple of messages from Annie. I didn't bother to listen to them and just called her. There was no answer. I left a message on the machine.

Annie was waiting when I got home. The kids, Jeff and Allie, were gone. Just looking at her I knew she was upset. The first thing I said was, "I'm sorry."

Annie turned heading for the kitchen. After hanging up my coat I followed her. She was putting my dinner in the microwave. "It is just that with you working and me working there's really only supper time to be a family with the kids."

"I know," I told her. "Maybe next year we need to go on a cruise."

She nodded. "Tomorrow night I want to go out, all four of us."

"Good," I said, "but could it be later?"

"Why?"

"I want to go out and see this patient again."

Annie wouldn't look at me. I could tell by her quick, jerky motions as she placed my supper on the table that she was upset. "Why?" she asked. "Why after all these years, when your family is home do you have to make a house call on this patient?"

"I don't know. I can't tell you why, but especially after seeing him tonight I have to go. It's something I have to do."

I looked at her. She looked at me. We held each other's gaze for a while. Then Annie came over to where I was sitting and kissed me on the forehead.

So the next night I headed out to Jim's without my black bag. Rev. Bill was just leaving. Jim asked me to talk about Annie and the kids. A different couple, Sylvester and Janice, were coming when I was going. I rushed off to a family dinner of garlic bread and pasta.

The next night Rev. Bill was still there. Jim asked me to talk about being a doctor. Ethel and Bob were coming in when I was leaving. This time it was the late show at the movies and pizza when we got home.

The fourth night was different. Rev. Bill was there. Jim asked me to talk about the future, my hopes and dreams. I had hopes and dreams once. It seems like they all came true, my practice, Annie, Jeff and Allie. Every other night it had been one sided. I would do most of the talking while Jim just gave me a verbal poke in the ribs to get me going. This time Jim did almost as much talking as I did. Every time he spoke there would be a delay as if he was tapping what remained of his strength in order to speak.

One of these silences stretched out. Finally, Jim said, "Time for you to be getting back to Annie." That was how he ended our talks every night so I did not think much of it. I told him that I would be back to see at the same time tomorrow night. He made some noncommittal remark. When I turned around Jim had his hand out. I took his hand. The grip was cold and weak.

"Good-bye, Dr. Ross," he said. "I want to thank you for sharing with me."

"Good-bye, Jim," I responded.

Jim let go of my hand and I left the room. There was no Ethel and Bob. There was no Sylvester and Janice. I hesitated. Perhaps I shouldn't leave. I looked at my watch. It was earlier than usual. Surely they would be along at the usual time. I decided to leave. It was not until I reached the highway that I realized Jim had said good-bye.

The next day was Good Friday. The office is only open half a day. I spent the morning waiting for a word, any word, on Jim. It came at noon while I was finishing with my last patient. The call was from Rev. Bill. Jim had died. Would I please give him a call?

I called the number on the note. After the usual hello's Rev. Bill asked, "Can you come by the funeral home tomorrow?"

I did not know why I should, but I knew I had to go. "Sure," I told him, "I'll try to make it by."

"That would be great. It would be really helpful if you could be there at the beginning of the viewing. We need to talk."

Again, I told him, "I'll try."

Over breakfast the next morning I told Annie I was planning to go to the viewing. Annie did not understand what was happening. That was okay. I did not understand it either. I had been a doctor for over twenty-five years and nothing like this had happened before. She gave me a look as if there was something she wanted to say and thought better of it. She went back to the paper. Rather casually she asked, "Do you want me to come with you?"

Actually, I did, but I had the feeling this was not going to be a quick in and out visit. "No," I said, "I think I'm going to be stuck there awhile."

I got to the funeral home about ten minutes early. The parking lot was already full. I had to park a couple of blocks away on the street. The line to get in the funeral home was out the door and down the block. I had no idea how many people came to something like this.

I got into line to wait with everyone else. Then I heard my name. It was Rev. Bill waiving from a side entrance. I left the line and went over to him. He took my hand when I reached him. "I'm so glad you could make it."

I turned to survey the scene. "I never expected anything like this."

"Now you know why I wanted you to come early," Rev. Bill told me. "There's something we need to talk about."

I did not really understand. I followed him into one of the few areas not overflowing with people.

"Jim placed his home and the store in a trust and made us co-executors," Rev. Bill said.

"Store?" I asked. "What store?"

"The store, the convenience store that Jim managed, he owned it," Rev. Bill said. "He never told you?"

"No, he never told me."

"Well, I didn't know about it until a couple of weeks ago. Jim always said he managed the store for someone else. When Jim told me he owned the store I asked him what all that business about managing the store for someone else was about. You know what he told me? That he managed the store for his customers."

Rev. Bill led the way into the largest room. He stopped next to the casket. Someone came up to him and shook hands. The next thing I know Rev. Bill turns to me saying, "And this is Dr. Ross, Jim's doctor."

The first person grabbed my hand. "Oh, Dr. Ross, thank you," she gushed.

I thanked her for coming, watched her go, and then another person was waiting to shake my hand and thank me. Looking up I see that a line has formed leading up to Rev. Bill and myself. I sighed, another surprise courtesy of Jim. I might as well make the most of it. I put on the best face possible.

The viewing was only supposed to last for two hours and end in a brief service presided over by Rev. Bill. We must have been there over three hours. I do not know how many people were there. It had to be in the hundreds. They weren't exactly the country club set. I knew quite a few, some patients, some relatives of patients, a few from the schools, and some from the hospital. Tom Miller the surgeon who had operated on Jim was there. They all thanked me. I thanked them all for coming. Some I assured Jim would appreciate their being there. And I did not understand any of it.

When the time came Rev. Bill took charge of organizing a brief service. He read several passages from the bible. The one I still remember is First Corinthians 13. At the end Rev. Bill said, "Jim, the man I knew and loved, had charity, was charity."

After the amens were said the crowd broke. I was too numb to move. Several people stopped by to take my hand once again. I mumbled what I thought were the appropriate words. Then only Rev. Bill and I were left. Bill said, "Thank you for coming, Dr. Ross. As you can see it was important for you to be here."

"Didn't Jim have any family?" I asked.

"No," Bill said. "There were no brothers or sisters. Mother and Father had died years ago. I would say that he was all alone in the world, but you can see that Jim was never alone."

We sat in the quiet for a minute. "Time for you to go home Dr. Ross. Your wife's going to be wondering where you are."

I briefly took his hand and said one more. "Thank you." Instead of heading for the door I went over to the casket. I put my hand on the casket. "Jim," I said, "what other surprises do you have for me."

The next morning was Easter. Annie, Jeff, Jr., Allie, and I were at a sunrise ceremony. It's a great way to start the day. Annie and I started coming as soon as we moved to town. We have not missed one since. There have been a few rainy days and at least one snowstorm, but on a day like this, blue sky with the early morning sun streaking the sky with yellows and pinks, it is just worth the effort. There is just a feeling of hopeful joy on such a morning.

I was sitting there with Annie at my side just soaking it all in. I could not concentrate on the service, but I had sort of a warm glow about the experience. The minister was giving his sermon. I heard him say, "…and Jesus died so that all mankind will find a new life," and it just sort of hit me with the beauty of it. I began wondering whether other religions have similar stories of sacrifice and hope. I just did not know. I had not taken religion seriously enough to find out.

I began to become agitated. I had to get out of there. The sermon ended. The congregation rose to sing a hymn. I grabbed my cell phone as if I had gotten a call, whispered in Annie's ear that I had to go, and headed for the door with my cell phone out so people would think I had an emergency. In the lobby I held the phone up to my ear and kept on moving until I got to our car.

When I got into the car I began to cry, no sobs, just tears and tears and more tears. I sat there trying to mop my face, hoping that no one would notice me. Then the car door opened. It was Annie. She just sat down and hugged me.

Later that week I was in my office sitting behind my desk. In the patient's chair sat a woman with breast cancer. She was in her thirties. Her mother had died at a young age of breast cancer. She had a ten year-old boy at home. The father of the boy was long gone. There was evidence that the tumor had spread. All the markers were wrong. I had just gone over the situation with her and she was having problems holding it together. Unusual for these circumstances, no one was with her.

I looked down at the desk, looked at that beautiful wood grain, and let my hand slide across the finish. In that moment, if I had an axe I would have chopped that desk into little pieces.

I stepped around the desk, grabbed some tissues, and pulled a chair up to face her. I was new at this. I always used the desk to keep my distance from patients. I did not want to get too close. I did not know what to say. Then I remembered Jim and the way he listened. I could try.

"I'm very good at what I do," I told her, "but if I'm going to help you I need to know something more. I need to know what is important to you. I need to know your story."

Christmas in July

I learned something about faith that day.

I was a child of the suburbs. So I found it a little strange that I ended up in rural America. After seminary I had spent several years as an assistant pastor. Then an opportunity opened to be the pastor of a church in the middle of farm country. Our local bishop called me up to say that I ought to apply. He thought it would be a good fit. I talked the situation over with my husband. We decided to apply and I got the job.

I do not want to refer to the town as 'small town' as that implies something that the town definitely was not. I would not call it a big town or small city as those terms imply something else. I grew to think of the town as the inhabitants thought of it, the right size for them.

I found it to be the right size for me. I had a lot of friends there. I delivered my youngest daughter there. I have great memories of my time there.

But there was one aspect of life in that town that I had not experienced growing up in the suburbs. In the suburbs people are worn out from fighting traffic during their commute. In the country the slower speed gives people the chance to pay attention to their neighbor. I tried to put a positive spin on that. I mean you have to admit it is nice to have someone worrying about you.

I was not surprised when some of my parishioners started telling me that something was wrong with Ted. He had gone off the deep end and I had to pull him back. I suppose that is part of the job description so I assured them I would.

Ted had lost his wife a few months before after a long illness. Ted and Marty had been long time members of the church. Every Sunday you could count on them being in church. That is until the last year or so. Marty was spending a lot of time in and out of hospitals. I visited her there fairly often. She had been a stalwart of various committees so she was missed. When the time came I presided at her funeral. Our little church overflowed.

A couple of weeks later I dropped by his house to see if there was anything I could do. Ted welcomed me into his home which was neat and clean. We chatted over coffee. He seemed in a cheerful mood. I thought he might have been preparing for his wife's death for a long time so that he was able to move on faster than many spouses I had counseled. When I left I told him that I hoped I would see him in church soon. Other than that I did not think I had anything to worry about with Ted.

The people in the church who were urging me to look in on Ted all told me to drive by his house after dark. Then I would understand. Ted lived on the other side of town so it was not an area I would pass through after dark. It was July so I had to wait until after 9:00 for dark. I packed the kids and my husband in the car to get some ice cream. There was a dairy bar we liked out past Ted's place. On the way back I had my husband Joe turn off the main road and head toward Ted's. When we turned down the street Ted lived on it was easy to make out. His house glowed like an amusement park.

Ted lived in a development of old fashioned ramblers on generous lots. Ted had used that generous lot size by filling his front lawn with every imaginable Christmas display. The house was outlined in lights. The detached garage was outlined in lights.

The kids thought it was cool. Joe, always a sucker for Christmas lights, stopped in front of the house. When a line of cars formed behind us he went down to the end of the block and turned around so we could pass the display again. When we left there was a long line of cars turning into this little side street.

The next day I called up Ted and told him we should talk. He suggested we get together the next morning. As I hung up the phone I thought Ted sounded great.

"Jen, thanks for coming by," Ted said as he ushered me into his home. "I've made some coffee. Let's sit out on the back porch and enjoy the day."

Ted himself appeared to be in good shape. He was tall with a full head of white hair that was neatly cut and combed. He wore a golf shirt and khaki pants. Both appeared clean and fresh. Ted had always been a smiler, someone who always found life a little funny. Being serious I am always a bit suspicious of people like that, but the last year the smile had disappeared. I was happy to see he was smiling now. In short I saw none of the signs of an individual deteriorating after the death of their spouse.

Ted ushered me through the house. The general color scheme was red and green. In every room there was a Christmas tree. In the family room Ted had set up a nativity scene. I stopped before a table covered with twenty or so miniature trees, none more than six inches in height, but all decorated with their own ornaments.

Ted was busy in the kitchen. "Do you like those?" he asked.

"Yes, very much," I told him.

"Marty collected them. I think her favorite was the one decorated with hearts. My favorite is the crystal tree in the center. I gave it to Marty for our fiftieth wedding anniversary. At night if you turn off all the other lights and just have the overhead spot on it gives off different colors as you walk around the table. It is really quite beautiful."

Ted appeared carrying a tray with a pot of coffee, mugs, and some cookies. As he led the way to the porch I peaked into the kitchen. There was no pile of dishes, no dirty pots and pans. I wished my kitchen looked so clean. As I followed Ted to the porch I wondered if he had a couple of widows looking after him. I had not heard any gossip, but it was summer so the word may not have gotten around.

We sat on the porch and Ted poured out. We discussed the weather, both kinds, hot and dry. I told him some of the gossip from the church. When enough time had passed I decided it was time to jump right in. "Ted, I see you are having quite a time with Christmas. Is there anything you want to tell me about?"

Ted's smile grew wider. He gave a little laugh. "Well, it has become a hobby of mine. I build all the displays in my workshop. I have a plot of the whole yard and I have planned a lot of additions to what you already see. But that is not what you really want to know, is it?"

I did not need to answer. I shook my head slightly knowing he would go on. "Fifty-four years we were married. I met Marty in high school. We got married in college. Everyone told us we were crazy. Everyone told us it wouldn't last. Everyone was against us except for my Dad. I think we liked the challenge. Fifty-four years, when you have been married that long you forget what the world was like before you met her. She was my world. And you know what? It was easy. Marty and I would hear about other couples having marital problems and we would just not get what the problem was.

"Well, it was easy until the last couple of years. Marty was diagnosed with cancer about five years before she died. There was some treatment the first year, but then she had some time when things seemed pretty normal. Then the cancer came back. She underwent some heavy duty chemo and the cancer went away. We had another period of things being pretty good. About eighteen months before she died the cancer came back for good. The frequency of doctor visits increased. For awhile she was in and out of hospitals, bleeding problems, anemia, pneumonia, other infections. We were always meeting new doctors being brought in as consultants. The experience was awful. At one point I went to my dictionary to look up the word 'clinical.' The second definition of clinical is dispassionate. Explained a lot. You could look up 'sterile' and find the second definition fitting better than the first.

"We were exhausted. Then a friend of Marty's, a good friend, suggested we see another doctor. Seeing another doctor was not what either of us wanted to do, but this good friend insisted so we gathered up the records and drove the fifty miles to this doctor's office.

"This new doctor was older and very thorough. He did a complete physical, spent time going through the records, asked detailed questions on what we knew about Marty's past treatment, and looked at the scans we brought. He did more. He asked about children and grandchildren. He took down their names, their ages, where they went to school, whether they were married. I thought it was just his way of being personable.

"When he had finished he left to see another patient telling us that his nurse would take us to his office where we would talk. We waited for him in the office. He came in apologizing for keeping us waiting. He sat down behind his desk He started to look through the chart again. As we waited I was getting upset that he had to review a chart he had just looked at, but now I realize he was trying to decide. At last he looked up from the chart and said, 'Have I told you I am going to die?'

"He held up a hand to stop us from saying anything then he went on, 'The difference between you and me is that you know your time is limited and you know what will cause your death. But you might outlive me. I could be T-boned driving through an intersection tonight. This weekend I am going to clean the gutters. Maybe my wife will be right and I'll fall off the ladder and break my neck. Maybe the stress will finally get to me and I'll have a heart attack while I sleep and wake up dead. The thing is I know life is not about how long you live. Life is about loving and being loved. When I see you and your husband, when I hear you talk about your children and grandchildren

I know that you have loved and are loved. I know you have had a successful life.

'So, the question is whether you have the motivation to try to get every last day or whether you have had enough of what I call the needles and nausea. One of the things I have found useful in deciding is whether there is some landmark event coming up, a birth, a graduation, an anniversary, which would give you a sense of completion. If there is we should go for it, pull out all the stops. If not then we can take another approach.

'You have some deciding to do. You do not have to decide now. You should go home, sleep on it. Whatever you decide I'll be happy to help you or your present doctor can work with you. She really is a fine doctor. Do you know what the hardest part of this job is? The patients you come to know best, the ones you admire and love because of their courage and hope, are the ones you lose. It really is a hard thing. I deal with it by embracing it, but most doctors put up barriers. You really can't blame them. The human heart can take only so much.'

"He asked us whether we had any questions. We had none. We had been coming to a decision for months. Marty died about three months later.

"When Marty died I was numb. I had been expecting her death for a long time. Still, I was unprepared. The kids came home. There was the funeral. The kids stayed about a week. I always love seeing the kids and grandkids, but I wish they hadn't stayed as long as they did. My mind was all fuzzy. I needed to clear my head. I needed to wake up.

"About ten days after the funeral I went to sleep early. I hadn't been sleeping well, not in years. This time I slept through until dawn. I woke up feeling great. The sunrise was spectacular. I came out here on the porch with my cup of coffee to enjoy the day. It was Spring. The flowers were out. The birds were singing. The endless change in the patterns in the sky was so beautiful. Then there was a glorious sunset followed by the stars. I stayed up late watching the stars cross the sky. When I finally went to bed I passed right out and woke up to a glorious sunrise. I spent that day the same way. And I came to some conclusions. I was happy Marty had died. I know that sounds awful. You don't know how much I would give to have her back for a day. She is the one thing I have never had enough of, but she was suffering. If you believe what I believe you know she is in a better place. The other thing I realized is that it is all a miracle, every flower, every tree, every bird. The clouds, the rain, the stars are all miracles. Waking up in the morning is a miracle. Every breath, every beat of my heart is a miracle. Having Marty in my life for even one day was a miracle. How can I not spend the rest of my life being thankful? Knowing that, if you believe what I believe how can I wait another day to celebrate the birth of my Savior?"

Ted stopped. I looked at him. He appeared calm. He was smiling. I did not know what to say. I suppose I could have told him that celebrating the birth of our Savior was something he should do in his heart everyday, but what was wrong with yard decorations? There were worse hobbies. The decorations gave a lot of people pleasure.

I finished my coffee. Standing I thanked him for the coffee and hoped to see him in church soon. I left him sitting on his porch. When I reached the car I sat there awhile looking at the Christmas decorations on his lawn. I guess I had been wrong. I thought that perpetual smile of Ted's was a sign of smugness. Now, I didn't know, perhaps he did know something the rest of us had better learn.

I drove away from Ted's home thinking of giving a sermon on not waiting to celebrate the birth of your Savior. I gave that sermon a couple of months later. Ted was in the congregation that day and we shared a smile after the ceremony.

A new job opened up. The pastor at a church in the suburb Joe and I had grown up in was retiring. I hesitated. I hated the idea of leaving my church, but the work opportunities for Joe were limited. I knew how much he wanted to move back near a city. Both sets of grandparents were old now. Moving would make it a lot easier to see them. So I applied, interviewed, and got the job.

The new church was bigger with more resources. There were more ministries and more missions. There was more of everything including people who thought they knew how to do my job better than I did. It comes with the territory. I did not mind. As much as I hated leaving my old church there was just so much to do at my new church that I was in heaven.

Joe and the girls were right at my side. At least that was what I thought until I had been there about nine years. The girls had left for college. One evening, one of the few evenings I had free, Joe comes home and wants to talk. He tells me that he has found someone else. He tells me that he admires the relationship I have with the church, but that is not what he wants, it is not what he needs, now. He ran into someone he dated back in high school and he just fell in love.

That was the end of twenty years of marriage. There was no recourse, no chance to change, no way to work it out. He was just in love with someone else. Surely I would understand because I still had my relationship with God.

Of course I didn't understand. I vacillated between blaming myself and being angry with Joe for not giving me a chance. I had trouble carrying out my duties at the church, but I soldiered on with a smile on my face. The one thing I could not do was couples therapy. I used to love couples therapy and now I felt like a phony who could not keep her own marriage intact. I even underwent counseling with a fellow pastor.

The worst part was the crisis of conscience. Joe was wrong. This bolt from the blue had so shaken my world that I questioned my relationship with God. I had always felt loved. Now I just felt cold.

It was July again. Almost a whole year had passed since Joe had shattered me. The divorce had been finalized. I was starting to put my life back together. I had spent a week at a church conclave. It felt good to be among colleagues, sharing stories, sharing prayers. I was driving home when I realized I was driving past the town I had lived in for ten years. On a whim I decided to have a look at my old church.

It was almost dark when I reached the church. I parked in the empty parking lot. I walked up and tried the front door. It was locked. What did I expect? I peered in a window. It was too dark to see anything inside the church. I walked around the building hoping to find some sign of life. There was none.

I was disappointed. I am not sure what I expected. I guess I hoped to stand once more in the pulpit. This church was the place in which I had been most at home with Joe and our two girls in the congregation. It was the wrong thing to think about. The sense of loss was so acute I started to cry. I ran to the car before anyone could see me.

As I sat in the car my mind raced with memories of my ten years at that church. Finally, it rested on one, Christmas in July. I had used the theme for several sermons over the years so I remembered Ted and his Christmas obsession fairly well. One of the reasons I returned to Ted's story was it made me smile. I could use a smile about then, but Ted must be eighty-five. Could he still be lighting up the July night? I would have to find out.

Ted's place was not hard to find. There was a line of cars heading toward a glow in the night. When it was my turn I found Ted's place to be gaudy and bright, but somehow heartwarming and endearing. Then I remembered the words of a man who had just lost the love of his life to a five year fight with cancer. If you believe what I believe how can I wait another day to celebrate the birth of my savior? And I smiled.

Christmas all Year Round

I was out of work again. Ten years, three start-ups, three crash and burns, I sure could pick them. No problem, I had always found work before. This time I might even try a more established company instead of a high intensity, high risk start-up. But the economy was looking like a crash and burn. Six months into my job search I had not found a job. I had been able to cover my half of this month's rent. There was no money left for next month. My roommate might carry me until he found another roommate, but that was all. After ten years I faced the possibility of living with my parents back in my old bedroom.

My girlfriend had even left me. I don't really blame her. We were not serious. We just went together for some laughs. I could not afford to hang out in bars or go to restaurants any more so she moved on.

I had been out that day knocking on doors, handing out resumes, following up on contacts. I stopped outside a café I used to frequent. I really wanted a cup of coffee. I got out the wallet and looked inside. Strangely enough the dollars had not reproduced since I counted them that morning. I sighed, put the wallet back, and turned away.

I heard a voice say, "Come on! I'll buy you lunch."

I looked around. There was an older gentleman standing at the door. His one hand beckoned me as the other held the door to the café. I looked at him and did not recognize him. My look must have said, "Who? Me?" because he said, "Yes, you. Come on. It's cold out here. I've got a story to tell you and this is not a pick-up."

He disappeared into the café. I was left there on the sidewalk. I thought about it for awhile. I really wanted a cup of coffee and lunch sounded even better. I entered the café and found him already sitting at a table.

When I came over to the table he did not get up, but extended a hand with a smile. "I'm Dan," he told me.

I took his hand and told him, "I'm Steve."

Dan looked around for a waitress, caught the eye of one, and gave her a wave. "Let's get our order in before we start talking," he said. Then turning to the waitress he said, "Martha, it's good to see you again."

"Dan," she said as if they were old friends, "don't see you much anymore."

"Well, now that I've retired I don't get into town much so I couldn't pass up a chance at lunch here. Steve and I need a couple of cups of coffee. I'll have the beef stew and a couple of those biscuits. And pie. Do you have blueberry today?" She nodded. "Good." Then he turned to me. "The beef stew is great here and you cannot pass up the pie. Don't worry about the check. It is all on me."

Now I had been living on cereal three times a day for the past few weeks so beef stew sounded great. I did not even want to look at the menu. "Sounds great, Dan," I told him.

Looking up at Martha Dan said, "We're simple enough."

Martha scooped up the unused menus. "I'll get the order right in and the coffee right out."

The coffee tasted great. It always did in that café. The stew was good, too. Not that I am any judge. I was always more of a salad kind of guy, but after walking the street on a freezing, cloudy February day I was happy to be eating something warm. The biscuits, split and buttered, were wonderful, but it got even better when Ted suggested some of the homemade preserves. "Turns it into a fruit course, don't have to feel as guilty," Dan said. It was delicious.

We talked as we ate. Dan was retired. The company's headquarters were around the corner, but they had a plant outside of town as well as a couple in other states. He was in his seventies and been married for forty-seven years. Every time Martha filled our coffee cups he said, "Thank you, Martha."

For my part I told him I was out of work. I thought there was no point in having pride any more. It is all about the networking. You never know who might be the right contact. Plus I really did not want to go back to my parents' house. Just the thought of living in my old bedroom with my parents and my older brother who never left home was enough to make me feel sick.

Dan was quite a talker, an expert really. He talked just enough to put you at ease and still left gaps in case you wanted to join in. By the time the blueberry pie arrived I was feeling pretty good or at least pretty full. I knew something about him, but not that much. I had told him more about myself than I would have imagined my telling to a stranger.

There was no story, though. That might have been a line, but I did not think so. Dan was too nice and too genuine to just use a line. I decided to change the topic from just conversation to us. "So, Dan, how did you know?"

"Know what?"

"That I needed this."

Dan smiled and gave a short snort of a laugh. "Well, it's my business to note such things."

"Really," I said, "that was what you did for the company you worked for?"

"I guess saying it was my business was not the right way to put it. It is really my life. You see a long time ago I resolved to do something for someone else everyday of my life. I wake up everyday looking for the opportunity to help someone. With that focus it is not hard to see the signs. A young man stands in front of a restaurant but does not go in. He reaches into one pocket, pulls out his change, looks at it, and puts it back. Then he looks in his wallet and turns away discouraged. I did not need a leap to think you could not afford a meal."

I hung my head. I was embarrassed that I had seemed so forlorn. "Don't worry," Dan told me. "No one else noticed. They are all to busy, but for someone who makes it his business to see such things the key was counting your change. No one counts his change in that situation if they have enough money. Besides, it is I that should thank you. You've given me someone to help today. And perhaps we are a lot alike."

I picked my head up and looked at him. Dan had a bemused little smile in place and was nodding his head. "Yes, I was once out of work and broke. A man befriended me and changed my life. This was back before I was married. It was a different world, but people are people. I was sitting at a lunch counter nursing a cup of coffee on another cold February day. I did not need to look in my wallet. I had nothing but three quarters in my pocket. The company I worked for had been bought the year before. Six months later they had fired everybody but some top brass. What we were doing they regarded as redundant. Jobs were scarce. I had not even had the hint of one since I was fired. I had managed to pay the rent the day before by selling most of my furniture. I had already hocked some personal items. I am down to wondering whether I really need a watch. The watch is a gift from my parents for graduation from college. If I am thinking of hocking that you know it is bad. I think I am headed back to my parents' farm, but right then I do not have bus fare. I feel really dejected.

"I was sitting there wondering if I could ask the waitress for another warm up of my coffee and whether I should put three or four packs of sugar in the cup. I wanted to take a few packs of sugar home with me, but I was afraid that they might consider that stealing. Suddenly a guy plops himself down on the stool next to me and says in an overly load voice, 'How about a cup of coffee and one of those donuts?' Then he turns to me and says, 'How about you? You want a donut on me?' And he said it just like that accenting the 'on me.'

"Now I'm so hungry my belly hurts. The only thing I've had to eat the past couple of days is coffee with cream and sugar so, of course, I say, 'Sure.'

"The waitress brings him a cup of coffee and refills mine. I opt for the four packs of sugar and fill it to the brim with cream. A couple of plates with a donut each land on the counter. I take a bite out of mine. I watch him break his donut in two and dunk it. He catches me watching him and says, 'Dunking a donut is one of the greatest pleasures of all time.' I thought I'd give it a try. I agreed with him. Dunking was okay..

"I am back to nursing the cop of coffee when he leans over to me and says, 'You know what I'd really like now?' He stops for a second, but does not really wait for my answer. 'That apple pie there. How about a slice of that pie on me? I mean, how can you say no to a fruit course?' I nod and he calls out to the waitress, 'Hon, could we have a couple of slices of that apple pie? And could you warm it up a bit and maybe put a slice of cheese on it. Thank you.'

"We get another refill on the coffee. I feel safe with three packs of sugar this time. The pie comes. We dig in. I think this was the best apple pie I've ever had. Probably had something to do with my state of mind and the needs of my metabolism. I was just cleaning up my plate when he leans over and says, 'I think I'd like a little more donut. What say we split one more?'

"After the apple pie all I could do was smile. I don't really need to answer him. He orders up another donut and when it arrived he slides the plate in my direction and says, 'Why don't you split this one?' I pick up the donut and split it. I do not make a very even split. I hesitate just a second and give him the larger piece. I must admit I feel a slight twinge of regret when I do so realizing that this last half of a donut is the last thing I might eat for a couple of days.

"Now everything he had said up until then was just a little too loud. This time in a voice slightly louder than a whisper he says, 'You gave me the larger piece.' Then he looked at me with this surprised look on his face. For some reason the quiet voice and the shocked look after the overly hearty conspiratorial demeanor of a few seconds before scares me. I start to apologize for taking the smaller piece. 'Don't worry,' he says in his quiet voice, 'it was the right thing to do. You know there are three kinds of people in the world. The type that takes the larger piece and the type that takes the smaller piece.'

"I ask him what the third type is and he tells me that those people don't even realize there is a larger piece. 'You,' he says, 'made a conscious decision to give away the larger piece. For a person that doesn't know where his next meal is coming from that took something. As a reward I am going to tell you the secret to happiness.

'There are two parts to the secret to happiness,' he says. 'Both are at the same time hard and easy. To make it work you have to put in the effort to develop the habit of mind so that over a long period it becomes easy for you. The first part is being thankful for everything. I can tell by the expression on your face that you have already thought of a situation you would find impossible, but I did not say it was easy. I also did not say that you could not feel sad or angry, but finding the sense of a situation that allows you to see it as part of the miraculous process that is this universe will allow you to overcome those feelings and remain happy.

'The second part actually helps with the first part, stop thinking of yourself so much and think of other people more. The best way to do that is wake up in the morning and make it your job to do something for someone else. Everyday I am on the lookout for something I can do for someone. I try never to think about my problems at all. When I have to solve them I will. The best part of this is you begin thinking of yourself as someone who has something to give. A person who has something to give always has worth.'

"I ask him, 'What can I give? I'm out of work and broke.'

"'Well, first, there's your time,' he says. 'Especially if you are out of work you have plenty of time. I can't help with a job, but I can help a little with being broke.' He stands up, reaches into his hip pocket, takes out his wallet, takes out all his money, and puts it in my hand. He holds my hand for a few seconds. Then he says, 'Merry Christmas,' and he walks away.

"I watch him disappear through the door of the lunch room. I am too stunned to say or do anything. I look down at the bills in my hand. I think counting them would seem ungrateful so I just stuff them in a pocket.

"After a couple of minutes I decide to go home and slip off the stool. A couple of steps later I remember the waitress. I put a couple of dollars on the counter and left the lunch room feeling pretty good about myself.

"The sun is going down fast and it is bitterly cold. It is probably just a caffeine and sugar high, but I feel chipper. I feel better than I had in months, maybe years. So, I wander around town looking at buildings and in shop windows, seeing things for the first time, waving to people, and saying 'hello' to strangers. Then I run into a panhandler. I give him a buck congratulating myself on my largesse, but after the panhandler shuffles off I realize something. If I gave every panhandler a dollar I will soon be broke. 'No fear,' I think, 'something will come along.'

"So, I continue my walk with a smile on my face and, yes, a song in my heart until I notice a group of people lined up in front of a building. I decide to check it out. Turns out it is a soup kitchen. Every night they give people a hot meal. I try to enter the building, but my way is rather abruptly blocked with some comments about waiting my turn until I tell them, 'I'm working here.' Then an opening appears and I am pushed on through

"I find the man who is in charge. His name is Abe. He is busy talking to some of the people having a meal. I wait until Abe notices me. Then I tell him that I want to help. Abe points in the direction of the soup line. 'See that girl with the pony tail over there,' Abe tells me. I nod. 'She'll put you to work.'

"I go over and stood where I think I am just in her peripheral vision. I wait for her to notice that I am there. And I wait. She is so focused in on what she is doing that finally I say, 'Hello,' to get her attention.

"I really am not prepared for what happen next. She turns to me with this thousand watt smile. Her lips, her eyes, her whole face are just lit up. I have never seen anything like it. The amazing thing is I found out this was low power for her. She can turn it up even more. I am so taken aback that I forget what I am going to say. I finally stumble over something about Abe sending me. She finds me an apron, hands me a serving spoon, and tells me what to do. She starts back to work. Suddenly she turns with a hand out saying, 'I'm Kate.' When I take her hand and manage to say, 'Dan,' I swear her smile went up a notch.

"I sneak peeks at Kate while we work. I do not want her to know that I am watching her. Some of the older guys in the line see exactly what I am doing and give me a wink. The smile is always there. Kate seems to know everybody. She speaks to them by name and has something special to say. The ones she does not know she introduces herself with, 'I'm Kate. You're?' No one can resist that smile. They all give their names. Then Kate thanks them for coming in and hopes they will enjoy the meal.

"I don't say much that first night, don't know how to fit in. When the soup line ends Kate says, 'There's some food left. When there's food left the workers get together and have a meal. You're welcome to have some.' I'm not going to say no to that smile. Besides, I'm like the people in the soup line. Two meals in the same day is heaven.

"Kate appears with two plates. She sets one down and motions me to sit there. I hope she will sit next to me, but she takes her plate down to the end on the other side of the table. Everybody else shows and fills in the table. I thank Momma for giving me the sense not to start eating right away. Everyone waits for Abe to sit down and say grace. After that everyone starts talking and eating at once. My neighbors introduce themselves, but I really don't get involved in the conversation. I am peeking down at Kate, trying to figure her out. The smile is there. She seems to be three to five years younger than I am, perhaps three years out of college. I try not to be too obvious that I am checking her out.

"When everyone finishes eating Abe asks, "Whose turn is it to clean the pots and pans?" I don't give anybody a chance to answer. I hop up, head back to the kitchen, and say, 'I'll do it,' on the way.

"Washing the dishes had been one of my chores growing up. Momma had always said that no one could do it better. Washing dishes became my thing so I started doing it at church functions, a ten year old kid in with all the adults cleaning up after a pancake supper. I had paid my way through college washing dishes. After college I swore I would not clean another pot or pan for money. That is a long time ago and cleaning up at the soup kitchen feels like being home again.

"After about ten minutes, when I am elbow deep in cleaning out a pot, Kate shows up and starts to dry. She does not say anything. I do not say anything. I do not even look at her. When she finishes she leaves without saying a word. I find Abe sweeping up in the dining area, thank him for letting me work, and ask if I could come back tomorrow. Abe tells me that they are always happy to have help, especially help that cleans up. I head home.

"The next day I spend checking want ads, walking the hallways of office buildings looking for a job. It is grinding work, but all day I think about working at the soup kitchen that night.

"I get there a little earlier. As the other workers show up I introduce myself and try to find something to do, but when they are ready to serve up the food I am standing next to Kate as if I own that job.

"She is as good as the night before, the same smile, the same courtesy. I am a little better. The night before I had been a silent Sam, tonight I am able to get out a few words of encouragement. Then we eat the leftovers. This time I just head back to the kitchen to clean up before Abe asks.

"The third night is like the previous two except when we finished serving I sit down with some of the customers. Turns out they are a lot like me. There are people who had ruined their lives with alcohol and drugs, but there are also people who had lost their jobs and still hadn't found work. I am looking down that same dark tunnel. Their spirits are still alive. They can laugh and when you see the ones with families you realize they can love.

"At one point I look up and see Kate watching me across the room. I look at her. For the first time I really look at her. Then I smile and nod and we both turn away.

"That night there are not any leftovers. We had more children than usual. The kitchen has a big sign saying, 'Children Get Seconds.' After I clean up the pots and pans I go home hungry. Somehow I do not mind.

"The next night something wonderful happens. As Kate serves the first customer she says, 'Bill, this is Dan. It looks like he's going to be with us for awhile.' Then she introduces me to everyone who passes through the line.

"Later that night Kate and I are doing our silent act while I wash and she dries when she asks, 'You seem to enjoy washing the pots and pans. Do you?'

"I tell her I do. Then I tell her how I had grown up washing dishes and how I had worked my way through college washing dishes. I tell her I promised myself never to wash another dish for money.

"Kate says, 'Still, you enjoy doing it here. Why?'

"I tell her, 'I guess this feels more like family.'

"Then Kate asks, 'Do you miss your family?'

"That brings me up short. I try not to think about it. I do not want to go back to the farm, especially as a failure, but 'Yes, I miss my family.'

"We are silent for a minute. Then Kate asks, 'Why are you so silent all the time?'

"The truth is that she intimidates me, but I cannot tell her that. So I say, 'I'm a stranger. I don't know where I fit in. Besides I get a lot of pleasure out of listening to the other workers. You're all so comfortable with each other. It is like a family.'

"That is the end of the questions for that night, but our sessions cleaning up become question and answer affairs with Kate doing the questioning. Soon Kate knows a lot about me, not the important stuff, not the way I feel about her, not how desperate I am for a job.

"About a week later, on a Friday, Kate and I are cleaning up when Abe pokes his head in the kitchen to ask Kate if she could lock up because he had to leave. I stay to help. When we had locked up I offer to walk her home. Kate will not have any of that. She does not need anybody's protection. Then we find out we are walking the same way. When we compare addresses we find out I live four blocks further along on the same street.

"We walk along in silence until we get to where she lives. It is a big old house. A lot of these had been converted to apartments like the one I live in. When we reach the walkway to the house I finally blurt something out, 'So, are you and your boyfriend going out later?'

"I know the answer I want to hear, 'What boyfriend?' Instead all I get is a, 'No.'

"Then I surprise myself. 'It's just that I can't see a drop dead knockout like you not having a dozen boyfriends hanging around,' I say.

"Kate turns and walks away. As I watch her head toward the house I know that I blew it. I wonder whether I should even show up at the soup kitchen again. Then Kate starts back. For the first time she isn't smiling. There is an air of determination about her. I expect to get slapped or worse. Instead she slips a hand behind my head and kisses me on the lips lingering for just a second. Our foreheads touch. We stay like that for a moment. Without a word Kate walks away and disappears behind the door.

"Well, I am dead in the water. All Kate had to do is reel me in. The problem is, at least in my own eyes, I am not a keeper. Right then I am fired with a determination to succeed. It is no longer about not going back to the farm. I had to succeed so that I can stay in the city and convince Kate to marry me. The problem is I am out of work, penniless, and have only two weeks before I have to leave my apartment.

"There is a gentleman at the soup kitchen that shows up to work most nights. Everybody just calls him John, but there is just the slight deference toward him from Abe and all the other workers. I have been there about a week and he introduces himself, asks what I've been doing lately. I tell him I am out of work and looking for a job and that I am working at the soup kitchen to feel useful while I look. Then he asks where I worked last. I tell him and I know that he knows exactly how long I have been out of work. A couple of nights later John says that he knows some people over at my old employer. I think it is just a 'who'd you know that I know' conversation, but looking back he asked too many questions about what my duties were.

"I have spent a fruitless week looking for a job since Kate had kissed me. I have the will, but my days before I have to leave the apartment were growing short. I am being ground down by the cold, the hunger, the frustration. I am so desperate that I am considering washing dishes again for money. If it weren't for Kate and the soup kitchen I'm not sure what I would have done. That night John sits next to me at the worker's meal. There are the usual pleasantries. Then John asks, 'How would like to work for me?'

"I cannot believe my ears. Before I have a chance to answer Abe speaks up, 'That's no fair, John. I was thinking of asking him to fill that financial position we talked about. Now I'll never find the right person.'

"After searching for over six months I have two job offers in a matter of minutes. I tell John just to give me the details of when and where and I'd be there. I look at Kate. She is looking at me. I head back to the kitchen before anybody sees my tears.

"Things are going pretty well. I like working for a paycheck again. I work late, but I manage to get to the soup kitchen so that I can at least clean up. John's company is pretty big. I do not see much of him at work. I have been there about a month when I see him down a hallway. He charges down calling my name, asks how things are working out. I can see a lot of people recalculating where the new hire fits. I am pretty sure that is John's intention.

"I see him at soup kitchen on a regular basis. I have thanked him for the job, but we never talk work until one night John says, 'I have heard great things about you at work, the long hours you have been putting in. Tell me how you like it. I would really like to know.'

"In the past I would just tell him that everything is great and thank him again for the job. I have changed. I tell him, 'I love working again. Being out of a job for so long gave me an appreciation of a good job, but I don't know who our customers are and how what we do helps them. I think I and everyone I work with would function better if we understood that. Maybe Abe was right. Maybe I do fit in better here. At least here I know who we're helping and how. And I've been thinking. Maybe I could start a job training program and find some of these people jobs.'

"After a minute of silence John says, 'Dan, please don't quit just yet.'

"I have no intention of quitting. I am frustrated. I love the immediacy of the soup kitchen. Every where I have worked seemed to be managed to make a profit even if it disadvantaged customers. I cannot do that anymore. John's company is no worse and probably better than most. I am not about to quit.

"About a month later I am called to see John in his office. As nice as John is, I really expect to be fired. This is a long time ago and no one talked to the head of a company the way I had back then. All I had ever said at my previous jobs were, 'Yes, sir,' and, 'Thank you, sir.'

"I get to John's office. John introduces me to a gentleman he calls Joe. I know him to be a senior vice president. John asks me to tell him again what I told him the other night about workers working better when they understand what they are doing for the customer. I tell them. It does not take long. Joe asks a couple of questions. I do my best to answer. Finally, John asks Joe, 'What do you think?'

"Joe answers a simple, 'I like it.'

"John looks at me. 'Dan,' he says, 'I was very interested in what you said the other night. I really believe in what we do here. I believe we create something of value for our customers not just make profits. Joe and I think that if we could get the whole company to understand that the company would work better and we would get a better product. I've decide that I want to make this a major initiative in the way we manage the company. We are going to focus on the customer and, yes, I expect to make more profits. Joe here is going to get that done. I would like you to assist him. It means a promotion and a raise. And when you get this part up and running we can talk about that job training idea you have.'"

Dan stopped talking a smile on his face. I sat there a minute in silence expecting him to go on at any second. At last I asked, "What happened next?"

"Well, the rest is history. As you can see meeting that man changed my life. Doing the right thing made me a success and ensured my happiness. It can happen for you. If you don't feel as if you have anything to give let me give you a start."

Dan reached into his pocket, pulled out a wad of bills, and placed them in my hands. Then he looked me in the eye, said, "Merry Christmas," and left the café.

I sat there a second before heading after him. I took two steps before remembering the waitress. I left a couple of extra dollars on the table and hustled after Dan.

I caught Dan down the block. "I can't take your money. It wouldn't be right."

Dan gave a little laugh. "You know that's the same thing I said. That's right. I went after him, too. I waited longer. When I got out of the lunch room he was gone. I ran to the left. I've found when you are on the right track you almost always turn the right way. When I reached the end of the block I saw him to the left crossing a street. When I reached him I tried to give the money back. That's when he told me what I am going to tell you. Because you came after me I know I made the right decision. Now it depends on what you choose to do with it."

"But what kind of story is that. The girl? What happened to you and the girl?"

"Oh! I decided I did not really deserve her and I tell her that every day. It's worth it to see that smile. So, Merry Christmas."

Dan started to go. Before he went I had to know. "Why 'Merry Christmas' in the middle of February?"

"That's another thing he told me. Life is about hope. In every act of hope there's a sacrifice. Think about it."

I let him go. Dan was half-way down the block when I yelled, "Merry Christmas!"

Miracles

"Idiot!" I had reduced my vocabulary to one word. "Idiot!" Every time I went in the bathroom I checked under my bangs to see if there was a red 'I' printed on my forehead.

It had been a week since I had used one of those home pregnancy tests. I had let out such a scream when I saw that it was positive that I am surprised the mirror did not crack. The timing was awful. I had been appointed VP in charge of marketing six months before. The company was planning a new software upgrade about the time I would be due. I was too old. After spending my life being prepared for everything I was not prepared for this. I was flying home for the weekend and I had a doctor's appointment in a few days. Perhaps the doctor would give me different information. The problem was it might be worse.

The doctor was taking off his gloves after the pelvic exam. He was rambling on about prenatal vitamins, diet, instruction sheets, and appointment schedules.

"How long do I have to decide?" I asked him.

"About what?"

"About an abortion. It is not something I am anxious to do, but I have considered it."

"I can't tell you," the doctor said.

"What do you mean? You just told me I was about eight weeks pregnant. You must know when the cut off time is for an abortion."

"I do, but I don't believe in abortion. I won't give you any information about abortion," he said.

"All I've asked for is a little information I can get off the internet. I respect the fact that you don't do abortions. I understand that you would not want to refer me to an abortion provider. I respect that and I am not asking that. I would understand and even appreciate if you wanted to counsel me against having an abortion. Instead you want me to make an uninformed decision. Really, where's the professionalism in that?"

The doctor just smiled and left the room.

I had not been home for over six months. I love my folks, but going home just feels a bit creepy to me now that I have lived alone for so long. I keep trying to get my Mom and Dad to visit me, but they have visited only once. I think the problem is my Mom. I think she is faintly uncomfortable with seeing her baby all grown up. At her house she has years of history that says she is the mother and I am the daughter. At my place she doesn't have that.

I am visiting for just the weekend so I just had a carry-on for the flight home. Dad picked me up at the curb.

"Where's Mom?" I asked. "She usually comes to the airport with you."

"Well, your Mom had some errands to run. She hadn't done any of the shopping for the weekend. So, I volunteered to make the trip by myself. Besides, you know me, I love driving on open roads, listening to music."

We were quiet for a while. The car slipped through traffic. In only a few minutes we were on the interstate, farms on either side of us. That was something I miss in city living, the sight of farm after farm, the acres of corn and soy beans, the silos, the barns, the farmhouses with their windbreak of trees. I had not grown up on a farm. Dad was an insurance agent so we lived in town, but the sight of the crops on acre after acre told me I was home.

"How's that new job working out?" Dad asked.

"Great," I told him. "I'm working really long hours, but I do that because I enjoy it. We have a couple of new products scheduled for release in six and nine months, though the way things work we'll be lucky if we get either of them out on time. Being in charge of the marketing is just the challenge I like so the extra hours are no problem."

"I was a little worried. You look a little tired. You need to take care of yourself."

We were quiet for a minute as Dad maneuvered around a group of eighteen wheelers. I looked through the passenger side window at the farms wondering what it was like to live under that open sky. I turned back to watch Dad drive.

"Dad, I'm pregnant."

Dad's face brightened for just a second then the smile faded. "I would say congratulations, but I gather that it is not altogether a good thing. Is there a man involved?"

"Of course, there's a man involved, but it is just a man I met on my trip to the Caribbean a couple of months ago that I took to celebrate the promotion. I work so hard. I love it, but it is still hard. And I'm always in control. I'm always sweetness and light, always in control, always supportive. I never let anything get to me. So, you know what? A few months ago, just after I got the promotion, a co-worker tells me that some members of my staff have nicknamed me 'the Iron Maiden.' She reassured me that they meant it in a good way. No matter what happened, no matter what the screw up, nothing would ever get to me. So, for all my efforts to be the best manager I know how to be I'm viewed as a thin layer of sweetness and light over a steel core. I was so tired of being in control. I just wanted to let loose. I didn't want to feel I had to be in control."

I saw Dad nodding as I spoke. He could not take more than a glance at me as he drove. He waited until he was sure I had stopped. "Shouldn't you be talking to your Mom about this?" I guess you don't sell insurance for all those years without learning how to read people.

"I can't tell Mom. Not yet, not until I decide what I want to do. If I tell Mom my pregnancy becomes her grandchild and I've lost control of my own body. I can't talk to Mom until I decide what to do."

"Don't you have any girlfriends you can talk to?"

"I work too hard and have risen too fast. The women I know are of two types, either married or still in the same job they had ten years ago. No, for them my pregnancy would just be gossip."

"Doesn't anyone else know?"

"Only the doctor's office."

"I guess I'm honored that you trust me, but I don't want to say anything that will replace my judgment for yours. I want to be helpful, but I am uncomfortable even with the idea of a decision."

"I know, Dad, but it's just that I have this fear that I may be ruining two lives. I know it may be irrational, but it's what I feel. On top of that I feel so alone."

Dad took his eyes off the road to look at me. Looking me in the eyes he said, "You know you are never alone," Then he turned back to the road and smiled. "Besides, you know your mother would do everything she could. She would just love another chance at raising a child. She'd be great."

I smiled, too. Mom did love her grandchildren. "Yeah, Mom would be great," I told him.

We were quiet again as we exited the interstate following a path I had taken a thousand times before. A few more minutes and we would be home.

"Dad, are you going to be disappointed in me?"

Dad gave me a quick glance and a smile. "Don't you know your mother and I regard you and your brothers as miracles? It is impossible to be disappointed in a miracle."

"Thanks, Dad."

We turned down our street. It seemed frozen in time. I know that at least the trees are bigger, but everything seemed much the same as when I was twelve.

"Dad, is there anything you do to help you make a tough decision?"

Dad waited until we had pulled into the driveway and stopped. After he turned off the car he said, "I guess I have been pretty lucky. I haven't faced a big decision in years. When I did I prayed. I know it is old fashioned, but I guess I am an old fashioned guy.

"Maybe we will get another chance to talk about this before you leave. We'll let your mother know about this when you are ready."

Dinner was not too bad. Dad had taken control of the conversation and kept it moving in directions that were safe. I had to hand it to him. All those years selling insurance and in Rotary had sharpened his skills.

After dinner we sat out on the porch enjoying the cool after a hot day. The fireflies were out. In the dark not much needs to be said.

I excused myself a little earlier than usual. In bed I tried reading a book, but I could not concentrate. A magazine was no help. I had business reports, but I was saving the reports for the flight home. Finally, I turned off the light and tried meditation breathing exercises to relax me.

The problem with the meditation techniques is that a lot of thoughts bubble up and you have to deal with them before you can get deeper. And there I was in the same bed with the same wallpaper and with the same curtains I had slept with since I was ten. Sleeping in that old bed always creeps me out. At least I had gotten rid of all the stuffed animals. Mom had kept all the stuffed animals I had collected over the years. Anytime I came home I had to share the room with the stuffed animals. There wasn't enough room for all of us in there. I got the idea of taking a couple back with me each time I left. I kept a couple in the spare bedroom in the condo, but most I gave away. That left just a huge bear that continued to stare at me while I tried to relax.

I lay there in bed trying to concentrate on counting my breaths and all the stupid stuff I did as a teenager. It was a wonder I was alive. Then I remembered Bobby Johnston. I hadn't thought about him in years. He had teased me all through fifth grade. I couldn't get him to stop and I couldn't get anyone to stop him. Finally, near the end of the school year he said something so horrible I hauled off and socked him. Bobby went down like a stone. He went down so hard and so fast I thought I killed him. I went from wanting him dead to wanting him to live in a second. When teachers grabbed me I was crying. They hauled me away to the principal's office. They kept on asking me what he said, but I would not tell them. I got suspended for the rest of the week. I had to spend all that time in my room. I was a little kid with nothing to compare this to. I was imagining the worst when Dad came into my room after he got home from work. He was carrying a couple of books he dropped on the bed. I'll always remember what he said, "Just got off the phone with Mr. Johnston. Bobby's fine. He might die from embarrassment being knocked down by a girl and all, but physically he's fine. I guess this just shows that there are all sorts of lessons to be learned in school. Why don't you turn off the light and get some sleep. You have had a big day and you will feel better after a good night's sleep. On Monday you'll be back in school. There's nothing to worry about."

I lay down. Dad pulled the covers over me. He turned the light off. I felt a kiss on my forehead and I slept.

The first day I was back at school I found a note taped to my chair. The note said, "Thank you for not telling what I said."

At the time it had all seemed so hard and scary. Now I can't believe how easy it was. I went back to counting my breaths. At last, I slept.

The next morning after breakfast I was curled up in an easy chair with the paper and a cup of decaf when Dad came in dressed for church. "You're not ready for church," he said.

"Aw, Dad, I just thought I'd be lazy and finish the paper."

"No," he said, "you want to come to church. Reverend Jen is giving her 'Christmas in July' sermon. You will enjoy it. It is different. She started giving the sermon a few years ago. Elly," he yelled over his shoulder, "how long has Jen been giving 'Christmas in July'?"

Mom yelled back, "The flier said this was the seventh annual."

Dad turned back to me, "The first year Jen gave the sermon it was just a sermon. Since then it has gotten bigger every year. Jen spends the whole year writing the sermon. It is something entirely different." Then Dad gave me a look and said, "You do not want to miss this."

As I headed off to my room to change Dad called after me, "And hurry! We need to get there early so we can get a seat."

Dad was right to have us hurry. The church was packed. They had even added extra chairs. I looked at the program and thought the service would be a short one. Some of the usual parts were missing. The sermon turned out to be the longest I had ever sat through. I don't think anyone noticed.

The Reverend Jen started out reading several passages from the Christmas narrative in the Bible. Then she said, "Christmas is a special time of year. There are Christmas trees to buy and to decorate. There are presents to buy. We are inundated with ads on television and in magazines for the perfect gift. There are trips to see loved ones. There are special meals and extra desserts and candy. It really is a time when visions of sugarplums dance through children's heads. It is a time when the world seems full of everything good and wonderful about life, but Christmas has become a time when it seems as if Santa Claus is more important than Jesus.

"I thought today, on the other side of the year, when the weather is least like Christmas, when there are no blaring ads for Christmas gifts, when we are not preoccupied with all the other things Christmas has become associated with we could talk about the meaning of the birth of our savior."

With that Reverend Jen left the pulpit and walked the aisles. She wore one of those microphones around her head so everyone could hear. People laughed. People cried. I have never seen anything like that in church.

There was one section of the sermon she referred to as about 'the birth of our lord and the birth of a baby' where she talked about the birth of her own children, a miracle of hope. My father was sitting on the aisle. Reverend Jen was standing near us when she reached this part. Her hand reached out and touched my father's shoulder. Her hand rested there just a second or two as if she was keeping her balance. Then she moved on.

After the service everyone was outside on the lawn. It was a brilliantly sunny day already too hot to spend much time outside, but no one rushed off. The woman's group had set up a punch bowl and cookies. Mom was busy introducing me to some of her old friends. They were names I remembered hearing, but they meant nothing to me. I saw the parents of some of my friends in school.

At one point I just wandered off a bit to be alone. There were a couple of young women talking. Nearby two men I assumed were their husbands were in conversation. What caught my attention were two children, a girl of about two and a boy a few years older. The boy was chasing the girl in and out and around the legs of the adults. The little girl was having a great time giggling as she went. Suddenly she took a wrong turn and ran into me. The giggling stopped. Her eyes got wide as she looked up at me. Then her mother scooped her up apologizing for her daughter.

"There's no reason to apologize," I told her. "She's a miracle."

On the way back to the airport Dad and I talked about baseball. He is a baseball fanatic and can spend hours talking baseball. I have been trying to get him to visit so we can go to a couple of games together, but it has never happened.

When we got to the airport Dad pulled up to the curb so we could both get out and say good-bye. After we hugged I asked him, "How come Mom didn't come along?"

"I found something else she needed to do and I told her I had a piece of business I wanted to take care of after I dropped you off. She decided she would have to forego the trip to the airport. Besides, I did not know whether you needed to talk some more."

"Dad, I wanted to tell you that I am going to call Mom later in the week and tell her I'm pregnant."

Dad smiled and hugged me. "I thought you had made a decision. You were smiling. When I picked you up you were not smiling. You do know this will change your life?"

"Maybe," I told him, "maybe that's the point."

Have you ever been in Love

"Have you ever been in love with someone else?"

"What kind of question is that? We're out celebrating our tenth anniversary and you're asking about other women."

"Well, you said I could have anything my heart desires. My heart desires to know more about my husband. Is that so strange?"

"When I said you could have anything your heart desires I had in mind a more participatory physical activity for couples."

"Oh, we'll get there after you take the sitter home if all three kids are asleep and healthy and if one of us doesn't fall asleep first, but what I want to know now is where the man who makes me deliriously happy, the father of my children came from. The first thirty years of your life are like a black hole. There's all this information in there that won't come out."

"That's silly. You've met my parents. You know the town where I grew up. You know where I went to college and medical school. You know where I did my training for psychiatry. You have all the facts. I was just another serious, focused medical student. There's nothing to tell."

"I'm not buying it. You're too handsome not to have been involved with someone at sometime in the past. Do you know how hard it was for me? I worked with you for a year. We talked everyday. I was hopeless the first time I saw you, but you were all business. You were so busy trying to be perfect I didn't think you even noticed me. Then one day everything changed."

Jack leaned back. Until then we had both been leaning over the table, sipping our wine in this outrageously expensive restaurant. Now Jack leaned back and gave me a look. The look was subtle. I had seen it before and I referred to it as his psychiatric look, noncommittal, rational.

"You know this is a very female thing you are doing," Jack said. "Guys don't care. Guys are interested in competitors. If there are no competitors there are no issues. Guys are much more in the moment."

"Oh, like you have ever been in the moment."

"Admittedly, I am not you're average guy. You do know that I've wondered what it would be like if we met in elementary school. Would I have dismissed you as just another stinky girl? Or how about high school? Would I have ignored you or turned you away with sarcasm? In college or medical school would I have even noticed you exist? As perfect as we are together I would have missed the best thing in my life if you hadn't been there at just the right time."

Okay, that was pretty good. Jack had a way of saying these things.

"Do you know what attracted me to you the first time?" he asked.

"No, you've never told me."

"You teased me."

"You mean I made a sexual pass at you?"

"No, though one could argue that all such repartee between a man and a woman has sexual overtones. I mean you teased me in the common sense of the word. You made a joke at my expense. I don't remember what it was, but it was pretty good sarcastic remark, not even said directly to me. And it was the first time I thought of you as anything but an administrator.

"And you know that business about me being attractive? I've never gotten it. I don't think I'm unattractive. It is just that body image thing that some people have. I just have never thought I was that attractive. Let me tell you a couple of stories. I did a medical internship. I was covering the CCU on Christmas Eve. As you might expect the nurses had a little party and included me. Someone had bought me a pen. I was really very touched that someone had included the intern. Then someone in a moment of camaraderie thought to tell me that all the nurses liked me, but thought I was too egotistical. I had never thought of myself as being egotistical before so the comment really stung me. I thought I was smart but so were all the other interns. Why had they picked on me? I came to the conclusion that it was my sense of humor. I specialized in sarcasm which was a typical form among my peers, but was deadly for anyone who could be regarded as a subordinate. So I kept my mouth closed and kept a strict adherence to our respective roles and probably made things worse.

"Then, a few months later I was working in the emergency room. I always worked hard. I didn't know how not to. It was about a month into a six week rotation, late on a Saturday night and I found two nurses looking at me. These were older women. I was a 26 year old intern and I now realize that they might have been all of 35 and probably not that. I asked them what the problem was and one of them told me that they couldn't decide whether I looked more like Cary Grant or Clark Gable. I didn't believe a word of it, but there was this look in their eyes as if I was a tasty morsel.

"The result was that in my interpersonal relations I retreated to treating the individuals I worked with according to their roles. I was, of course, objectifying them, but what was worse was that I was objectifying myself."

I had enough. I held up my hand to stop him before he could get into a full blown lecture. "I give up, Professor. I was wrong. I want my husband back."

Jack smiled. "I told you this wasn't a subject for an anniversary."

"I just can't believe there wasn't someone else. I know that under the Professor there is a deeply passionate man, warm, caring, human. I just thought that after ten years of marriage and three children it would be safe to know what makes you tick."

"You make me tick. I thought you knew that."

"More evidence of why your eyes are brown if you ask me. So, I guess that's all."

"That's all for tonight." Jack changed the subject to our plans for a summer vacation. But Jack had said tonight. Did that mean there would be some other night? The Professor never used stray words.

The rest of the night went well. The kids were all asleep when we got home and we found time for a little participatory physical activity for couples.

I really forgot about our discussion that night until about a month later I was in the basement looking for a book. We moved into the new house a couple of years before. We still had boxes and boxes of books that we had never unpacked. Jack and I loved books. We could never throw out a book. I was opening boxes searching for a copy of Twain's 'Innocents Abroad' when I came across Jack's high school yearbook.

I hesitated. Maybe I shouldn't. I ended up forgetting about Twain and spent the afternoon leafing through the yearbook. I found Jack's picture. He really hadn't changed that much in over twenty years. He was the captain of the cross country and track teams. I had never known that. There were a lot of people who had signed the yearbook. There was one that was different. Her name was Kathleen and she signed herself as Katy. She didn't write anything about remembering science class or when they were in elementary school together. She just wrote, "Love is eternal. We are forever." Remembering what Jack had said I thought, "So, you're my competition."

I did not approach Jack right away. I was not sure I should approach Jack about Katy. I was a little scared about what I might find out. I buried the yearbook under some sweaters until I could decide. A couple of times I went back and looked at Kathleen's picture. It was the only picture of her in the whole yearbook. She was not drop dead gorgeous, but she was cute. I think I could have handled drop dead gorgeous better. The attraction might be only physical. I was worried there might have been a deeper bond. Jack worked that way.

After thinking about it for a month I decided I had to know. How bad could it be? I could forgive Jack anything. The question was whether Jack could forgive me.

I waited until a Saturday night at home. When the kids were in bed I poured us a couple of glasses of wine. I handed Jack one and he gave me a quizzical look. I handed him the yearbook. Jack looked at the yearbook and then looked at me. I thought about what I was going to say for awhile. I did not want it to sound like a shrill demand. I wanted it to be a request that Jack could refuse. But I did not want him to refuse. I was dying to know. I said, "Jack, please, I'd like to know about Katy."

Jack gave me a wry smile and without opening the book said, "Love is eternal. We are forever. You do know I can say that about us?"

I did not say anything. Jack patted the sofa next to him. "There's a storm coming in. Let's watch it. Maybe we'll talk about it after."

I sat down and he put his arm around me. We did not have long to wait before the storm rolled in. It was quite a show, a little scary. Even when a bolt of lightening struck right in front of us Jack did not flinch. I held him closer.

When the storm was over Jack took his arm from around me and picked up the yearbook. He did not open it, just held it. "You know this is so like a woman. A guy will take a car or a watch apart to find out how it works. A woman has to take a person apart mentally. A guy could care less."

"So said the psychiatrist."

"Fair enough. You know I used to run. I loved to run. There was such a feeling of freedom. Striding along, gliding over the ground, it was like flying, so alone with the rhythm of my stride, so perfect. There was nothing like it. It was all I was really interested in when I was in high school. I was a disappointment to my father. My grades were okay. Science and math were no problem, but I always got marked down because I couldn't bother to do homework. English was another problem. It was so subjective that my problems with authority cost me more.

"Then there were girls. I had a few dates, but basically I wasn't interested. I either ignored them or teased them with sarcastic comments. Mostly I ignored them. Then there was Katy. You know I haven't looked at this yearbook since, well, since then. As I remember the picture did not do her justice. She was a real cutey. At least I thought so. It was really something about the eyes. She had these bright blue eyes and dark hair she wore in a pony tail. Her eyes were lit with delight. They came alive when she smiled and she had a lot of smiles. I think the one I liked the best was the smirk she used when she was needling me.

"I met Katy in English class. She was sitting next to me. It was the last class of the day. It was the only class we were in together. She was new to school having just moved into town over the summer. Naturally, I didn't even notice her until our teacher was passing back an assignment when she made a perfectly sarcastic remark about our teachers intelligence. When she noticed I was staring at her she made a sarcastic comment about me being the spoiled son of a rich doctor. I was hooked. Here was a challenge. Here was a girl I might get and, more important, might get me.

"We talked after class, not for long. I always had to get to cross country practice. I started showing up late to practice, definitely not the behavior of a team captain, but I had problems pulling myself away. This went on for two weeks or more before I asked her out. Katy refused, claimed her parents would not approve, but she did study every night at the library. I remember her asking, 'You do study, don't you?' The truth was that no, I didn't, but the next Monday night I was at the library.

"Katy was a whiz at English, but struggled with math and science. Those were easy for me. I spent more time tutoring her than I'd ever spent on my own homework. With my tutoring, Katy didn't have to spend all night on math and science so we had more time to spend on English.

"I said Katy was a whiz, but it was more than that. It was her passion. She had already read all of Shakespeare and everything we were reading for senior English. Katy introduced me to poets and dramatists I had barely heard of. One night when we had finished all our work we found a corner of the old library where we could talk. There, in hushed voices we acted out scenes from 'Hamlet' and 'Romeo and Juliet.' I know it sounds corny, but it was a great experience. Katy was a fair Ophelia and an even better Juliet.

"The amazing thing was that the world was different for me. I was different for me. I didn't think it at the time and I probably never said it to myself until later, but it felt like I had found the one. We hadn't dated. We hadn't kissed. I suppose every case of young love feels that way, but even now, twenty-three years after the last time I saw her I remain convinced she was the one.

"Each night I tried to drive her home and each night Katy refused. She usually had some sarcastic comment about the spoiled rich kid with a car. I felt so ungallant letting her walk home alone in the dark, but she wouldn't even let me walk her part way. I had an idea where she lived. It was the other side of town from where I lived, but it was not far from the library. After weeks of begging her to let me drive her home she told me that if her parents thought she was seeing someone at the library she would have to study at home. Besides, she couldn't give up her tutor with finals only weeks away.

"Christmas came and I couldn't see Katy, no school, no reason to go to the library. I wanted to call, but Katy said her parents would not like it. I told her to call me. Katy said my mother wouldn't like that and I told her I didn't give a damn.

"So, for almost two weeks I went without a dose of Katy. I was miserable. I couldn't wait for school to start. There in English class I realized something had changed. I wasn't sure what it was. I couldn't wait for class to be over so we could talk. It turned out things had changed. She had missed me as much as I had missed her.

"We went back to the same routine for awhile, but we both knew it couldn't last. Typically it was Katy who made the first move. One night after studying in the library we had said our good-byes and Katy had walked across the parking lot when she turned around and yelled, "You're not much of a date. We've been seeing each other for months and you haven't even tried to kiss me. I'm beginning to wonder whether you like girls." Then she turned and went.

"I made Katy wait a week. I told her there was something I wanted to show her down one of the aisles in the library. I led the way through the stacks. When I had her in position I turned and kissed her before she could react. I was worried that if I signaled my intentions Katy would laugh. After that first kiss I said, "My God, why did I wait so long?" and kissed her again.

"I should never have kissed her. Before that we were just pals sharing a cynically sarcastic view of the rest of the world. After the kiss we were lovers. It was good thing we met in a public place because I couldn't keep my hands off her. I would have spent every second of every minute we were together kissing and holding her. I couldn't get enough. I never got enough.

"It's sort of funny. I had been meeting her at the library for about two months. There was another couple there not doing any work, just staring at each other across a table. We both noticed them. Katy turned to me and said, 'If you ever look at me like that I'd have to shoot you.' To which I responded, 'If you ever look at me that way I'll die of surprise.' As a psychiatrist I now know we meant, 'Please, look at me that way. I'm dying to have someone look at me that way.' Now we were worse than that other couple.

"It was a good thing we were entering the second semester of senior year because I was useless. Katy was so used to grinding away that she kept us close to the straight and narrow. If I had my way I would have given up studying entirely.

"I only remember a few things about that semester. The first is that Katy let me read her stories. I thought the stories were good. They were touching and tender and funny. They made me look at this girl who was an expert at the sarcastic put-down in an entirely new light

"Then there was 'Hamlet.' The senior English class studied 'Hamlet' during the second semester. Our teacher made everyone memorize a certain number of lines. We could either write them or, for extra credit, recite them in front of class. Katy convinced me to recite the lines. I was going to do the scene with Ophelia where 'Get thee to a nunnery' comes in. The plan was that I would need someone to read Ophelia's part. Katy would volunteer and help me get through it. We rehearsed it. The day came and I got up to recite much to the amazement of the teacher. I ask for a volunteer to read Ophelia. Nothing happens. I steal a glance over at Katy. She has her head buried in a book. Finally, the teacher asks for a volunteer. Katy still has her head in the book. Just when the teacher starts to say that she will read for me. Katy looks up and waves her hand. With that sweet voice she used on teachers and an innocent smile she tells the teacher she'd be willing to help out. Katy comes to the front of the class carrying her copy of 'Hamlet.' Now she gets into an argument with the teacher whether reading that scene means reading from the entrance of Ophelia or should it include the 'To be or not to be…' speech as it really is the same scene. I'm standing there listening to Katy debate the teacher about what I need to do for extra credit. Katy knows I know the speech. She's yanking my chain because she knows she can. The teacher is clueless and my friends in the back row are starting to break up. Finally, I give up and agree to start with 'To be or not to be.' So, angrily I tear into the speech and I look at Katy. She's got her head down so all I can see is the top of her head. When we reach the time for Ophelia's entrance suddenly she looks at me with such intensity that I choke. I literally could not speak the line. Katy gave me the line again and I was able to stumble through to the end with something sounding like profound regret. It had turned into a love scene instead of a brush off. And Katy had her laugh at my expense. Somehow I did not mind.

"Then there was my mile against the best miler in the state. There was a big region-wide track meet coming up. The coach had run the numbers. If we could place in the mile we might win. The problem was that our top miler was out. The coach asked if I would run the mile. Being a team co-captain I could not say no even though I hated running the mile. It was too short. I considered my self a marathoner running track to stay in shape. I didn't even like competition that much. What I really liked was training. I got up every morning at five to run for an hour. After school I worked out with the team. Weekends were the best. I could run for hours.

"I had spent the week talking about the coming track meet. I had never asked Katy to come to one of my meets before. She'd try to be there. On the day of the meet I was scouring the stands hoping to see her. A little before the mile I saw Katy sitting high up in the stands. I waved to her. She waved back.

"Now in the mile there are two basic strategies: go out early and try to hold on or wait until sometime in the last quarter mile to sprint to the finish. I wasn't a sprinter. At the beginning of the race I went to the front. I had no feel for pace so I just tried to keep ahead of the field and concentrate on the rhythm of my stride. I was zoned in that day. I could really feel the rhythm. My feet barely felt the ground. I didn't hear the crowd or my teammates shouting encouragement. It was just me and the few yards of track in front of me. At the end of the first quarter I picked up coach and he gave me a hand signal to pick up the pace a little. The coach gave me the same signal at the half and three quarters mark. I expected to be in pain, struggling to breath and to maintain the rhythm of my stride on the last quarter. None of that happened until after I crossed the finish line with a win by twenty yards. I was gasping for air and the first thing I did when I regained some control was look for Katy. She wasn't there. I can't tell you how disappointed I was. Then I heard her voice. Katy had moved down to be next to the track. I went over to where she was and thanked her for coming. She said that she would never pass up a chance to see me sweat. And I gave her a kiss. It was the first time I'd done anything like that in public. Turns out she had been at all my cross country and track meets and I never knew.

"It was after graduation. My parents went out of town for a week. Katy and I had not been getting together as often as there was no more need to go to the library. Katy had taken a job waiting tables which kept her busy at night. I had a day job for the summer doing real guy things like lifting heavy objects and moving them from one place to another. I convinced Katy to come over to my house after work for awhile. We made love that night. She came over two other nights and we made love then, also.

"It was wrong. I know that now. It was wrong and those three nights were as close to heaven as I will ever get. I'm sorry. I know how that must sound to you. I was younger then. My experience of life was much more direct.

"The rest of the summer was unsatisfactory. Katy worked. I worked. I'd try to see her after she got off work. I would pick her up and drive around for half an hour before dropping her off near her home. We didn't really talk that much. All I know is how I felt when I saw her. I'd see her and smile. She'd see me and smile. Life was better if only for a little while.

"I quit my job a week before I was to go to college. Katy wasn't going to college. No one in her family had ever gone to college. What an absurd waste. She had to go to college so she could teach. Katy assured me she would take some community college courses. In the meantime she would continue writing.

"I was lying down in my room trying to figure out how I was going to communicate with Katy. I couldn't call her because her parents wouldn't like it. I didn't even know whether I could write to her. It must be so much easier now with cell phones and e-mail. Then my mother knocked on the door. A girl called Kathleen was on the phone. I didn't think of Katy as Kathleen so it took a second. Katy said that she wanted to be sure I picked her up that night. We had to talk.

"I picked Katy up at the restaurant. She attempted a smile. I knew something was wrong. She suggested we park near the library and talk for awhile. We drove over there in near silence. I was expecting the good-bye speech. High school is over. You'll forget me at college anyway. I parked the car and waited. I couldn't even look at her I was so scared of what she was going to say. Then she said, 'I'm pregnant.' She had been to a clinic. A doctor confirmed it.

"The next thing she said was that her parents were going to kill her and I saw something for the first time, fear. I have seen it since in my patients who have been subjects of abuse. It doesn't matter whether the threat is real or imagined. The fear is real. I should have known. The signs were there. Her hands, those hands that I had kissed a thousand times, had scars that were typical of cigarette burns. During the year she had a few bruises I let her explain away. I should have known, but I was just the spoiled rich kid going around destroying a life.

"I didn't miss a beat. I asked her to marry me. I knew what I wanted to be. It would be the challenge of a lifetime, but isn't that what life is about, finding someone and making a life with them. It would be hard, but I was up to the challenge. I wanted her. I wanted the baby. I wanted the challenge. I wanted it. I wanted it. I wanted it.

"I like to think my father would have supported us. The psychiatrist, the hyper-rational man, studying teenager americanus in the flesh, so much more interesting than in books, would have found reason to support us.

"My mother would never have accepted Katy. My mother would always look at Katy as the thief who stole her son's life. She'd never be able to see that Katy was my life. Here's a question: What is more important, going to medical school or being with the one you love?

"So, what do you think I got for my proposal? A laugh, it wasn't a bad laugh and after the look of fear I saw in Katy's eyes it was a welcome change. She refused. We fought. We never fought. I pleaded. I begged. I threatened. I wanted her to come with me that night and get married. I'd drive wherever I had to so we could get married.

"At last Katy said she had to go. She asked me to hold her and kiss her like I meant it. That was not hard because I always meant it when I kissed Katy. When we had finished kissing she got out of the car. Before closing the door she leaned back in and said, 'Don't look so sad. You're going to be fine.'

"I watched Katy walk away. She turned, gave a smile and a wave like she always did before disappearing. I thought, 'I'm not giving up.'

"I spent the next day at the library looking up the laws regarding marriage. I went by the restaurant where Katy worked at closing time.

Katy wasn't there. The next day a friend called. He wanted to say how sorry he was about Katy. I didn't know what he was talking about. It was in the morning paper. Katy had died in a one car accident the previous evening. I was devastated. I couldn't breathe. I wasn't sure I wanted to breathe. I had planned a life with Katy in it. I had proposed. We had a baby. And now?

"There was a viewing the next evening. I did not really want to meet Katy's parents now, but I needed to see Katy one more time. I went at six. There weren't many people there Katy's family being relatively new in town. Katy's father wasn't there. Seeing Katy's mom was like seeing Katy with 25 years, 40 pounds, and a million cigarettes. I shook her hand and told her that I was sorry for her loss, that Katy was special.

"The casket was closed, but someone had done a color blow-up of the yearbook picture. Seeing that photo made me weak and I reached out to the casket to steady myself. My eyes were getting wet. I needed to get out of there before I totally broke down. On the way out I received a few hugs and well wishes. I had to leave. They were only making it worse.

"When I got home I changed into running gear. It was not unusual for me to go for a run in the evening particularly in the summer when the days were hot, but I had given up running at night for Katy. It felt so good to be running again, the breeze against my face, alone with the rhythm, always the rhythm of my stride.

"I started out to the east side of town. I liked to run a series of hills there. I did one circuit and it was as if I was called back to town. I ran to the library and ran around it three times. I remembered Katy's smile when she saw me the first time I came to study with her. Then I headed for the block where she lived. The newspaper had included an address in the article about the accident. I ran around her block three times. The last time the thought of never seeing Katy again hit me like a punch in the stomach.

"I lost that feeling of rhythm and glide that made running feel so free. I kept on running, but it was like I had gone too fast and too far. The joy had gone. There was nothing but effort as I headed west out of town, west where thunder rolled and a storm brewed.

"I had been running west for about half an hour when the first raindrops hit. The rain was gentle at first, but within a few minutes there was a downpour. Still I ran. I had no clue as to where I was headed. I had no idea as to what could make me stop. I had no reason to go back. Then I passed the road to the old quarry. When I was twelve a group of us guys would ride our bikes out there and sneak through a break in the fence. It was a good place to throw rocks around. I headed up the road.

"I had to slowdown to a walk. The road was in poor repair and the only light was the occasional flash of lightening. I found the gate and felt my way along until I found the break in the fence. I managed to squeeze through. A flash showed me the way to the old timekeeper's shed. Beyond that I edged forward until a flash showed I had reached the edge of the pit. I stood there looking down into the pit, a black abyss with outlandish shapes lit only by lightening. The worst of the storm swirled around me. While electric shocks passed through my body I knew just one step and I could join Katy. At last I threw my arms out to the side and held them there. I looked up to the heavens. The rain poured down, the lightening flashed, the thunder roared, and I yelled as loud as I could. I had no idea why I did that, but I kept yelling until my voice broke. Exhausted I stepped back, kneeled down, and prayed for forgiveness.

"I woke up with first light and walked back into town. My mother was angry that I had given her such a worry. My father took a look at me and suggested that I clean up and put something on my bleeding knees.

"My father came into my room late that afternoon. I had gotten a couple of boxes and was removing everything that had to do with running, every medal, every trophy, every poster, even the shoes, shorts, and shirts. He came in but didn't say anything about that. He said, 'A young lady by the name of Kathleen called here a few days ago.' I didn't answer. Then he said, 'I saw in the paper that a girl by the name of Kathleen died in an auto accident. The paper said she graduated with you. Did you know her?' I couldn't answer. Finally, 'Was Kathleen special to you?' I had my back to him when I answered so he couldn't see the effort I made not to break into tears. 'Yes, she was.' There was a pause. Then I felt his hand on my shoulder. 'We should talk about this when you are ready.' I wasn't ready. His hand squeezed my shoulder and he left.

"Two days later I was at college. I tried to be perfect. I got good grades and I got into medical school. I worked and I worked and I never ran again. In the end I couldn't make a joke. I couldn't even look at a woman."

Throughout that whole story Jack had held the yearbook without opening it. Now he put the book down and gave it a little shove as if to say "The end." I put my hand around the side of his head, kissed him on the temple, and laid my head on his shoulder. We sat quietly looking into the night.

"What are you thinking?"

"Does this mean that the psychiatrist's back in charge? Are you through channeling the eighteen year old?"

"Well, the eighteen year old is still in there, a little closer to the raw surface than he's been for awhile, but the psychiatrist would probably ask, 'What are you feeling?'"

"I'm feeling sort of sad for the eighteen year old. I liked him. I probably would have fallen for him, but he probably would have broken my heart if he even noticed me. Mostly, I'm feeling sad that the barriers we erect to protect us most often destroy us. The eighteen year old never had a chance. He didn't really know Katy very well."

"I thought I did. There were parts of her I knew very well, but I was probably projecting my thoughts on to her. Everyone does a little of that. I've found that projection doesn't really matter unless it matters. The problem is that it always matters at the most inconvenient time."

"There's the psychiatrist again and he's avoiding the most important question."

"And what would that be?"

"Were you forgiven?"

"I can't speak for God, but I should have died that night. The wind could have blown me over the edge. I could have slipped and fallen into the pit. I should have been hit by lightening. I was so wet and cold when I woke up that morning I'm surprised I didn't get pneumonia. But, if you want the real sign of forgiveness it was finding you. When I found you I felt alive again."

"And you? Have you forgiven yourself?"

"Ay, there's the rub. I've never been able to get over the message in her last words to me. Katy said, "You'll be fine," not we'll be fine or everything will be fine. I can't get over the feeling that if I followed her home that night, if I had barged in and told her parents that she was pregnant, that the baby was mine, and that I wanted to marry her I could have saved her. Katy would be alive today and I would be with her. What was the worst that could happen? Her father might have beaten me to a pulp. It could not have hurt worse than what I went through. Then, when I trained to be a psychiatrist and learned about reading cues I started to realize the cues were there for me to read. If only I had understood the cues Katy was sending I might have saved her. I've spent thirteen years remembering and now I've spent ten years forgetting. I've learned that I had to put Katy behind me, but, no, I've never been able to forgive myself."

We were quiet again. With my head on Jack's shoulder and his arm draped over me I was strangely at peace despite the story of Jack's and Katy's tragic love. There was nothing for me to forgive, but Jack the perfectionist would never forgive himself even if time allowed him to forget. I had not helped by asking him to remember.

"Do you know what I think?" Jack did not say anything. "God is more forgiving than man. If you have to be perfect why don't try being perfectly forgiving and start with yourself."

All Jack said was, "Yes, Dear."

Be Silent

"Ali, are you alright?"

I was leaving the office on a Friday afternoon after finishing my paperwork when I passed the office of my junior partner. He was sitting at his desk with his head in his hands. Ali took his hands down so he could see me. "Jeff, I'll be fine. Are you leaving for the weekend?"

I stepped into the office. "You don't look fine. Is there something you need to talk about?"

Ali answered by motioning to a chair in his office. I sat down and waited for him to continue.

"It has been a tough week," he said, "too many emergencies, too many hospital admissions. The real problem is that a patient of mine died today. She had been one of my first patients when I arrived here. I had taken care of her for over five years. She was about my age. I had met her husband. One time she had her kids in the office with her. She had not been doing well, but one day she got sick and the next day she was dead. I've never lost a patient that I've treated for such a long time. In residency and fellowship you don't get to see patients for more than a few weeks. I'm stunned."

Ali was a good soul. Despite what some of our patients think when they hear his name he was born in Chicago and was a diehard Cubs fan. He was a good fit for our practice.

"Let me tell you about an experience I had as an intern. I spent three straight months on the cancer ward. Whoever made out the schedule knew of my interest in oncology and thought that would be a good idea. It almost drove me out of medicine. It was a different era then. One hundred hour work weeks were the norm. On that rotation I just had a lot of sick people. It got to the point that I felt like beginning my histories with 'This is the final hospital admission.' I had a lot of successes, but a lot of them died. I felt I was surrounded by death. I was a one man war zone. I wasn't prepared for it. I don't think anyone could be prepared for it.

"It got so bad that every morning the first thing I would do was check the discharge and transfer book to see whether anyone had died during the night. It was late in my three months on the cancer ward that I caught one of our attending doctors going to the discharge and transfer book first when he came onto the ward. He acted as attending for all the unassigned patients so he had a lot of patients in the hospital. I asked if things had gotten that bad and he said that yes, they had. Then he said, "Jeff, it's not your fault." I appreciated him saying that, but I still had to live through it.

"One of the problems of being on the same ward for so long was that some of the patients I had worked like a dog to get out of the hospital and back to their families two months before were getting readmitted. If it wasn't my turn for taking admissions my senior resident would often accept the patient on the theory that I already knew the patient.

"I was on my last week on the cancer ward when one of my old patients showed up. I wasn't on call, but my senior resident accepted the patient for me. I was not amused even though I liked the patient. He was a lawyer about ten years older than I was. He had been fighting a lymphoma for over five years. None of the usual medications worked. We had spent sometime talking about malpractice cases. This time he was really sick. He had miliary TB.

There was no apparent worsening on morning rounds, but by noon he was dead.

"I was on call that day. My ward had more open beds than any of the other wards so I was swamped with admissions. At 2:00 am I was still working. I went down to the vending machines to get a cup of coffee with my usual double cream and double sugar thinking I would have to stay awake for another hour or so.

"Near the vending machine was the hospital chapel. I had gone in there a couple of other times during internship. The chapel just seemed a good place to get away for a few minutes.

"I had always felt at home in churches. I came from a family where Sunday was the center of the week. After college and medical school I had become a man of science. The answers to questions being given by religion just didn't speak to me. But it was more than that. Medicine taught the ultimate in humanist values, the individual human life over all. But it was more than even that. If the ultimate sin is man being so prideful that he wants to become God what is more prideful than thinking you are defeating death with your own skill?

"So, I go into the chapel with my cup of coffee. I sit in one of the back pews. I close my eyes and drink my coffee hoping to know a little peace before I head back to work. I'm tired. I'm lonely. I'm confused. I'm depressed. All the death I've seen over the past three months has me questioning whether I belong in medicine. I lean back against the pew and my right hand bumps into something. It is a Bible open facedown on the pew. I pick it up and notice that someone has highlighted a passage. I silently wonder who could have done something like that, closed the Bible, and put it back in the rack. Then with the curiosity typical of a doctor I wonder what the passage was. I thought it was Psalms so I turned to that section and flipped the pages until I found the highlighted passage. I believe it was Psalms 46:10. Here is what it said: 'Be silent and know that I am God.'

"I read the passage and I read it again. I read the whole psalm a couple of times before putting the Bible back. I wondered whether some other intern or medical student with our ubiquitous yellow highlighters had sat right where I was experiencing a dark night of the soul. I went back to work to do what I could, all that I could, knowing that it was not everything."

I had finished my little story. We sat there in silence until I looked at my watch. I had not realized that it was so late. "I've got to be going," I told Ali. "Sarah wants to go to a movie tonight. Try to get some extra sleep this weekend, hug your wife and kids, and get some exercise. I find those things help with job stress."

I got up and reached the door when I heard Ali say, "Jeff, thanks."

Management

"No wonder they call you a saint."

I shouldn't have said that. I was meeting him for the first time. I had been with the company about six months. My boss, Mr. Telmar, had handed me an envelope and told me, "I want you to find Lawson. He's not in his office and I need an answer on this right away." If Mr. Telmar couldn't find him I was not sure I could. I headed for Mr. Lawson's office as a starting place for my search.

Every company has gossip spreading about higher-ups. Who is a good boss? Who is a bad boss? Who do you want to work for? Mr. Lawson was the one everybody wanted to work for. He had this reputation for, well, perfection that was not believable. I thought, "If he really is that good why doesn't he manage a division? Why isn't he an executive VP?" Still, I wanted to make a good impression.

Mr. Lawson's secretary told me that his wife and daughter had been there. If I hurried I might catch him at the front entrance. I ran down three flights of stairs and into the lobby. At the security station I asked the guard if he had seen Mr. Lawson. The guard pointed to a man behind a wheelchair. "That's him right there," the guard said.

I took a couple of steps toward the door and stopped. A van had pulled up and a woman had gotten out. The crippled little girl held out her arms as if she wanted to be picked up. Mr. Lawson bent down and picked her up. It was more than just a transfer from wheelchair to van. Mr. Lawson hugged the little girl and kissed her. The little girl hugged and kissed back. The wife had come around to open the passenger side door. Before they placed the little girl in the van she put her arms around both of them. Now, I am a typical young guy who watches sports and blow'em up movies, but there was something very human and tender in that scene that gave me pause.

The van had driven off and Mr. Lawson was striding past me so fast I almost let him get away. "Mr. Lawson, I'm Robert Stevens and Mr. Telmar wanted me to give you this and wanted an immediate reply."

Mr. Lawson took the envelope and continued down the hallway. I fell into step beside him. He opened the envelope and read the contents as we walked. For some reason I felt the need to say something. That is when I said, "No wonder they call you a saint."

Mr. Lawson stopped. The look he gave me could only be called stern. I was contemplating what I could say next that would not get me in more trouble when he smiled. "Walk with me. I think you could use a cup of coffee."

We did not say much as we headed for the cafeteria. We got our coffee and donuts with the minimum of words. Mr. Lawson bought and headed for a table by the window. When we had taken our seats he said, "Hold on a second," and took out his Blackberry. After sending a text message he said, "I wish people would stop saying things like that. I'm going to tell you what really happened."

"I met my wife at a charity event. You had to see her then. Hair, makeup, clothes, everything was perfect. She was a corporate lawyer and I was a hot shot young manager with this company. I saw her at the bar. I watched her for a while expecting her to be with someone. When no one showed I went over and introduced myself. The first thing she said was, 'If you waited any longer I was going to have you arrested for stalking.'

"We hit it off right away. Eighteen months later we were married. For awhile we lived high, fancy vacations, fancy restaurants, fancy clothes. Then we decided to have a baby. We were both a little apprehensive about what a baby would do to our lives. We had no idea.

"We were lucky. Janet got pregnant right away. The pregnancy seemed to go well. Janet went past her due date. The delivery was what they call 'post-term' and was complicated. The baby ended up in the neonatal ICU. There were heart problems that necessitated surgery. There was a chromosomal problem. The first few weeks were hell. I didn't think we were ever taking the baby home, but eventually we did. It was then real problems began.

"Having a new baby is real work, but our child, Marie, needed a lot of nursing care. Janet went right after it. I kept telling her that we could hire a nurse, the money would not be a problem, but she just looked at me and said, 'This is something I need to do myself.' After I had suggested hiring a nurse a couple of times I gave up.

"Then the date for Janet to go back to work came and passed. Janet hadn't mentioned that she wasn't going back. I had always assumed she would be going back. I brought the issue up. Janet gave me one of those looks that said I thought you knew and then she said, 'I thought you knew I couldn't leave my baby like this.' It was the end of any discussion.

"Taking care of Marie was taking a toll on both of us. By the time I got home at night Janet was exhausted so I had to get to work caring for Marie. The change in Janet amazed me. This woman who had always been impeccably dressed now lived in jeans and a tee shirt. Makeup was a thing of the past. I don't think either of us ever thought about making love. We were both too tired. The only together time we had was when we slept next to each other and there wasn't much of that as Marie seemed to need one of us all night long.

"Taking care of Marie was taking a toll on my job. I was so exhausted I fell asleep in a couple of meetings I had called. I was also missing a lot of work for doctors' appointments. We had a pediatrician, a cardiologist, a cardiac surgeon, a neurologist, an ophthalmologist, an orthopedist, and a physical therapist. Every week I missed time from work.

"This had been going on for almost a year when I was called in to see the VP I reported to. He was not amused. He had been receiving poor reports on me and our latest project was behind schedule. Unless I could give him some answers he was going to replace me. I assured him that the issues were behind me and I would meet the schedule.

"I had always considered myself to be a hot property. Everything I had touched had turned to gold. I was so good I dragged the rest of my team along with me. I had risen fast in the organization and had designs on becoming CEO one day, but I wasn't sure I wanted to wait that long. I had several friends who were considering start-ups and wanted me along with my money for CEO. I had one friend in particular that had a great idea for an app and had actually created a test version. He was a programming type and wanted me to be CEO of his company.

"With the birth of Marie and all her problems all my career dreams had disappeared. I hadn't seen anyone in that crowd since the birth of Marie. Now my job was falling apart. I walked out on Janet and Marie.

"I know. I was a real heel. That's why I don't like people talking the way you did. If they knew the truth they would never forgive me. I've never forgiven myself.

"I got an apartment downtown not far from the office. I still paid all the bills, but Janet and I never talked. Everyday I expected to hear from Janet's divorce lawyer, but nothing ever happened.

"The first few months I went out at night, a lot catching up with old friends. The friend who had the idea for an app told me that when I was no longer available he had sold it for millions. Most of my other friends had moved on and I realized so had I. I even went on a couple of dates, but they ended up being just polite and unrewarding. In the end I just sat in my darkened apartment watching the city lights.

"I had left my wife and child for about a year when I received a message from Janet. It said, 'Your daughter is going to have surgery at Children's on the 17th at 9 am. Perhaps you would like to be there.'

"Janet's note created a crisis for me. Ever since I had left Janet and Marie I had been working at a high level. My star was on the rise and I had just been offered a new project. The problem was I couldn't go on like this. I wanted to go back, but I hadn't talked with Janet since just after I left. Shame, really. I didn't know whether she wanted me back. Then if I did go back there was the problem of the job. I didn't know what to do.

"All this was running through my brain one morning while I was heading to the cafeteria for a cup of coffee. On my way I noted an older gentleman who seemed to be lost. He must have been close to ninety. I asked him if he was looking for the cafeteria and offered to buy him a cup of coffee. He told that he liked to sit in the cafeteria and observe the employees. 'It gives you a feel for the place,' he said.

"We sat down over coffee and donuts just like we are now. I have to admit the old guy was pretty good. We hadn't been sitting there more than a couple of minutes before he had me talking about my problems. He was a good listener and, having all this on my mind, I probably said more than I should.

"Suddenly he laughed. I was a little angry that my problems should cause him to laugh, but before I could say anything he said, 'I am sure glad I do not work anymore. You kids now-a-days are all in such a rush. You think it is all about making money or becoming an executive vice president or even CEO when it is really about the work. Take the man that built this company. I know for a fact that he had no idea that he was building this company. He thought he was making products to help people. And he did believe in his product. The key was that he always hired people he liked and he liked the people he hired. Now find work that is worth doing, work with people that inspire you, and work to inspire them and you'll find the rest of the problems will go away. Maybe you will never become CEO, but you will have a better life.'

"He paused here. I had a feeling he was not through so I waited for him to continue. Finally, he said, 'I am sorry to hear about your daughter. I hope everything works out for her. Marriage is another problem, but you can approach it the same way as work. Find inspiration in the ones you love and work to inspire them and you will find the rest of marriage is easy.

'Now as to your problem with work here at the company and your responsibilities at home I suggest you go up right now and talk to Jim the CEO. If he is not in make an appointment as soon as you can. I think you will be surprised at the result.'

"I found myself getting up from the table and heading for the executive suite. I had reached the exit to the cafeteria when I turned around, went back to the old man, took his hand, and said, 'Thank you.'

"When I reached the CEO's office I was getting cold feet, but on the way up there I had decided that I was willing to quit my job to get back with my family if my family was willing to take me back. The CEO's assistant told me he was on the phone and asked me to wait. I paced back and forth rehearsing what I was going to say. Ten minutes went by and the assistant told me I could go in.

"I entered the office to find Mr. Sever, the CEO, standing behind his desk with his hand extended already thanking me for coming in. Introductions were made and he motioned me to sit and asked what was on my mind. I went into my story about Marie and how that had affected my work. I told him that I thought I had proven my value to the company and that I could go on having value for the company, but not at the expense of my family.

"Mr. Sever listened and when I was finished he was quiet. Then he said, 'Give me a minute,' and turned to his computer. A couple of minutes later he turned to me and said, 'The project you have been assigned is very important. It is the only truly new product we will be introducing next year.'

"With those words my heart sank. I knew the next thing he would say was that it was too important for someone who had family problems. Then he went on, "This is what we are going to do. You will still have to report through Mr. Lee, but that will only be a formality. You will put together your own team instead of one assigned to you. You can work with anybody in the company if they are willing to work for you. If you put together your own team and cannot find people to cover for you maybe you are not as good as you or we think you are.'

"Mr. Sever stood up and extended his hand. The session had been short, but it was everything I could have hoped for. I left already plotting who I wanted on my team.

"The next day I was late to the hospital. Marie was already in surgery. I entered the waiting room and stopped. Across the room sat Janet. I had not seen her in over a year. She wore jeans and a plain top. Her hair was pulled back. Her head was down reading a magazine so I could not tell if she was wearing any makeup, but I would guess very little. Gone was the slick corporate lawyer. In her place was a strong woman capable of deep love. I had been so lucky and I had thrown it all away.

As these thoughts raced through my brain Janet suddenly looked up and smiled. It was not the huge smile that made me fall in love with her, but at least it was a smile. It took my breath away.

I walked over and sat down next to her. My mouth was so dry I could barely mumble an apology for being late. We sat there, upright, staring across the room, not daring to say a word. Out of the corner of my eye I could see her hand resting on her leg. I put my hand on top of hers and managed to choke out, 'Please, take me back.'

"Janet turned her hand over, laced her fingers in mine, and said, 'I've never let you go.'

"Well, it was all over except the kissing and hugging. I moved back in the same day. I've considered myself to be the luckiest person I know ever since, but you can see why I don't like people calling me a saint. I know exactly how egotistic my actions were. I was a heel, plain and simple."

Mr. Lawson drained his coffee and stood up. "Sit there and finish your coffee," he told me. "I've already e-mailed Mr. Telmar the information he needed and I told him I needed you for a little while so he won't be angry when you get back. There's just a couple of things I want to tell you so you don't have to learn them on your own. The experience made me a better manager. Instead of doing everything myself I was forced to rely on other people. I learned to respect their skills and help them succeed. Most of all I learned to trust. You know what trust means, Stevens?"

"You mean you trusted the other members of your team," I told him.

Mr. Lawson smiled. "Well, that's sort of the idea, but there's a bigger team and on that bigger team they call it faith. You take care, Stevens."

As I watched him walk away the only thing that came to mind was that from my tiny corner of the corporate world he certainly sounded like a saint to me.

Jan

"Jan, what's wrong with you?" Tina had entered my cubicle where I was having lunch.

"What do you mean?"

"You know what I mean. In the meeting this morning when Murray started with his stupid ideas you didn't cut him down to size. When Jack asked for volunteers to help Bruce on his project you actually volunteered. Bruce is a lazy louse who'll let you do all the work and then he'll take all the credit. You've never put up with Bruce before."

"It's no big deal," I told her.

Tina pulled up a chair and sat down. She pulled a sandwich out of the bag she was carrying and started to eat. Around bites from her sandwich she continued to talk. "Yeah, it's a big deal. The only pleasure I have in working here is watching you chew up and spit out all the idiots around here. What am I going to do if you go all soft on me." Then Tina looked around, leaned over, and whispered, "You've had sex. Isn't it? It's either that or a new boyfriend, maybe both. C'mon, tell me what's happening. This is Tina."

Tina was the only friend I had at work. We often had lunch like this. I heard all about her dates, usually in more detail than I wanted. I knew about her Mom's illness and her brother's stupid girlfriend. She knew all about Jeff, my ex. Jeff and I had been engaged and living together. One day we are planning a wedding and the next Jeff is out the door. The only thing he said was, "You're no fun anymore." That was almost three years ago. I've not had a boyfriend since.

I put down my sandwich and drank some of my soda before answering. "It's no big deal. I just had a dream last night. That's all."

Tina sat back. "That's too bad. I was hoping it was sex. I mean, I know how long you've been out in the cold. I'd rather hear about sex, but it must have been some dream. So, tell me about it."

"When I left work yesterday I headed for the health club. I was just about to start my workout on the elliptical when who should enter the room but Jeff. He was laughing and carrying on with a girl of about twenty, almost half his age. Our eyes met for a second. He smiled, said something to the girl who turned around and looked at me, and escorted her from the room. I got on the elliptical and started to go. It was obvious that he had told that girl about us. I was burning with rage. As I worked out the anger drove me to go faster and longer than I had ever worked out before. When I stopped I was totally drained."

"You know you're a little crazy," Tina said.

"Yeah, but if you want to hear the story you cannot interrupt."

"Needed to be said."

"Okay. When I got home to my apartment I was too tired to eat. I was too tired to do anything. I just got in bed with all my clothes on and pulled the covers over me. Then I started to cry." Tina started to say something, but I held up a hand to stop her.

"I was just so tired of hating, of being angry all the time. It was burning me up. And I really wanted to find someone new. I want to love someone, but every time the anger comes out and I end up cutting them down to size. It's really my size I cut them down to. I'm the small one. I just didn't know how to change.

"I fell asleep crying. When I woke up the pillow was still wet. I was disoriented. I had to look around the room to be sure where I was. Then I felt the call. I had to go somewhere. I left the apartment and headed over to the park near my building. I seemed to know exactly where to go 'cause I found an older gentleman sitting on a bench under a light.

"Now when I say he was older I don't mean to say he was unattractive or elderly or old and wrinkled. No, he was distinguished."

"Sort of like Mr. Stevenson," Tina added.

"Yeah, I guess."

"I knew it. That Mr. Stevenson is kind of hot for an older guy. He must work out. I think he has a lot of money. And he hasn't remarried since the divorce."

"Tina, it wasn't Mr. Stevenson. I'm trying to tell you the story of my dream. It is tough enough to get through without your interruptions. If you can't be quiet I might as well give up."

Tina took a noisy draw on her soda and said, "Sorry."

"I hid. I knew something was going to happen that I was supposed to see. Shortly, a young man showed up, well dressed, handsome. He was too handsome, really. The type women swoon over. There was a strange light about his eyes. His perfection was at once scary and attractive.

"The young one walked right up to the old one and said, 'There you are, Old Man. I've been looking for you everywhere.'

"'Then you must have found me,' returned the Old Man, 'for I am everywhere.'

"The Old Man's voice surprised me. I was expecting something loud and commanding. Instead it was quiet and calm. As I think over the rest of the dream I think that was the greatest impression I had was of a great calm that you could almost wrap yourself in.

"Anyway, the Young One told the Old Man, 'Enough of that Old Man, you know exactly what I mean.'

"The Old Man returned, 'I see that you feel I have not been properly solicitous of your difficulty. Perhaps you would like to take the time to tell me of your efforts.'

"The Young One started telling him of the deals he was working. How with the present economic crisis the world needed his skills more than ever. He went on and on about economic growth curing the ills of mankind. It reminded me of a presentation that he had rehearsed for just this moment. As he talked he paced and became self-absorbed.

"While the Young One was talking the most marvelous thing happened, the Old Man began to change shape. Old, young, male, female, different races, the Old Man changed into one right after the other. It was the most incredible sight. I lost all interest in the Young One. His speech became background noise as I watched this spectacle as in a trance.

"Suddenly the Young One stopped. Staring at the Old Man the Young One said, 'Will you please cut that out?'

"The Old Man passed through a couple of more forms before returning to the form that I first laid eyes on. 'I forget that you feel comfortable with only one form of me. Very well.'

"The Young One was exasperated. 'You have not heard a word that I have said.'

"The Old Man returned, 'I have heard everything that you said or do you doubt whom you have found?'

"The Young One said, 'I know who you are and you know who I am, Old Man. Now, you have heard all my efforts on behalf of humans, my accomplishments. What have you done for man lately?'

"For the first time the Old Man gave a little laugh. 'Why, everything, of course,' He said.

"The Young One almost jumped out of his skin. 'Everything! Everything, you say. Then I have you. Humans suffer. More humans suffer now than ever before and you do nothing about it.'

"'This is something you have never understood,' the Old Man said. 'It is humans' nature to suffer. Humans are also capable of great joy. The greatest joy comes when they overcome suffering through love. These are things you have no knowledge of. They are totally foreign to your nature due to your flaw.'

"'My flaw,' the Young One said, 'my flaw, how can you talk of me being flawed. I am the most perfect of creatures.'

"'You have defined perfection as you,' said the Old Man. 'That is so typical of your problem. You have too much pride. You have too much ego. Everything that you do you are doing for your benefit, not humans'. Your pride prevents compassion. It is the only way you can grow.'

"'You dare to call me uncompassionate. What do you know about suffering, Old Man?' said the Young One.

"There was just a few seconds delay. Throughout, the Old Man had a look of pleasant forbearance. Now there was a sudden look around the eyes of disappointment. 'I see you have forgotten already,' the Old Man said.

"The Young One waved that off with the back of his hand and stomped away. Then he whirled and pointed at the Old Man. 'I sought you out to tell you that your magic is dying.'

"The Old Man answered, 'My magic, as you call it, can never leave the universe. Its message is too strong and too simple. Fear not, you are loved is the message. It can never die.'

"'Yet, there are more followers of me than ever before,' the Young One said.

"'If it is mere numbers you are interested in, there are more believers in me than ever before,' said the Old Man.

"'More of the intelligent ones follow me,' the Young One said.

"'That is because you have defined intelligence as following you,' the Old Man said.

"'There are even calls for the idea of you to go away. What do you say about that?' asked the Young One.

"'I agree with that,' answered the Old Man.

"The Young One danced with joy. 'Oh, finally to hear those words, you don't know how long I have waited.'

"'Your pride gets the better of you again,' the Old Man said. 'To be an idea, a concept that can be limited and controlled by words on a piece of paper or thoughts in a mind, a thing to be used as a bludgeon on an opponent, that is not what I am. I am the experience of life, terrifying and glorious, quiet and sad, hopeful and joyful. And the message is fear not, you are loved.

"'You seem doubtful, as you always are. Perhaps I could show you something tonight, something that will show you the magic still existing in humans. I will perform no miracle, yet a miracle will occur. I guarantee that the outing will have features of which you approve. I will even give you a free hand to intervene if you desire.

"'A fieldtrip,' the Young One said, 'by all means, let us proceed as long as you promise not to perform one of your magic shows.'

"The Old Man said, 'The only magic will be the human heart, but I need one more player.' Then the Old Man turned to me. 'Little One, yes, you come out here. Have you heard nothing? Fear not, you are loved. It was meant for you. Come out. That is better. You have been paying close attention to everything we have said. Perhaps you would like to join us on our little outing?'

"I nodded and the next thing I knew the three of us were sitting at a table in a bar. It was a quiet night. The bar was only half full.

"'So, who is our subject for the night?' asked the Young One.

"The Old Man told him, 'Tom, the one in the middle.'

"The Young One thought that was hilarious. 'Tom! Tom is one of mine. Oh, this is going to be rich.'

"'I thought you would approve,' said the Old Man. 'Tom is truly a lost soul.'

"'What is wrong with Tom,' I heard myself say.

"The Young One answered, 'Let me tell her. His wife divorced him a few years ago. Ever since he has been trying to kill himself with drink. He is doing a pretty good job of it. A couple of more years should really wipe out his liver, but if he is lucky he will die sooner than that in a car accident or falling down a flight of stairs.'

"The Old Man shook his head. 'It is a little more complicated than that. Tom remembers a day that was filled with hope and a young woman who looked on him with adoration. That was perhaps the best moment of his life. Twelve years later he was married to a woman he still adored, but she knew too much to adore the man that he was. She left when she found someone else she could adore for the moment. He comes here or another bar most every night to forget and he chases women to remember. And, yes, most of his time is so filled with pain that he would like to die.

"'That is our introduction to Tom. We only need the highpoints of his time in the bar. Let me speed things up a bit. Note the several drinks that he orders. Watch as he flirts and strikes out with a series of women. No luck for Tom tonight. Tom gets up to go. He appears a little wobbly. The bartender tries to prevent Tom from leaving. Tom angrily pushes the bartender away. Exit Tom.'

"The Old Man turned to me. 'I was wondering. Does he remind you of someone?'

"I said, 'Jeff.'

"The Old Man nodded and said, 'I thought he might. Hate him, do you?'

"I said, 'Yes,' but I was not sure whether I meant Tom or Jeff.

"'Let us look in on Tom in the parking lot,' the Old Man said.

"Suddenly we were standing in the parking lot. The Young One was looking in a car window. 'He's asleep,' the Young One said. 'I can't believe this. He should be out driving, causing mayhem. With any luck he could get his wish and die in a car accident tonight.'

"Then turning to the Old Man the Young One said, 'This is your doing. You are trying to protect him. When I agreed to come you promised that you would not try one of your magic shows.'

"'Indeed, I have not,' the Old Man said. 'I guarantee that before this night is over you will be pleased and,' here the Old Man turned to look at me, 'perhaps disappointed. We have seen enough here. Let us move on to Tom's next stop.'

"We found ourselves outside a convenience store. Tom's car was at a pump. We were only there a few seconds when Tom emerged from the store with a cup of coffee in one hand and a half eaten donut in the other. The Old Man spoke, 'Let us forego any comments on his choice of snacks and move on to Tom's next destination.'"

"We ended up at a deserted country crossroads. I was the first to speak. 'Why are we here? There is nothing here.'

"The Old Man looked at me. 'Nothing, Little One?' He said. 'I suggest you look around now because you do not have long before there will be more activity than you like.'

"Even as we spoke I saw two head lights in the distance. Turning I saw a couple of sets of lights on the crossing road. They seemed to approach in slow motion until they were right next to me and then in a flash there was a terrific crash as one car hit the other broadside.

"'Yes!' it was the Young One shouting in glee. 'Yes, yes, yes, yes, yes, yes, I must admit, Old Man, you do deliver on you promises.'

"The Old Man turned to me. 'Come with me where we can get a better look. There you see how Tom's larger vehicle has pretty much crushed that smaller car. As you see most the point of impact was right where the driver sits. Tom was saved by his air bag. Now here he comes. The door manages to crack open and he pushes his way out. He falls to the ground upon exiting the vehicle, but now he struggles to his feet. He looks at the other car. He sees the other driver, a young woman, not moving. He races to the other side of the car. The doors are locked. He returns to his car and pops the trunk. Tom pulls out a golf club. He returns to the other car and smashes the window with repeated stokes finally using his hand to clear the glass. He opens the door and reaches in calling out to her. He touches her neck and waits. He slumps in the passenger seat covered in glass. Now listen to his wail. He has not lost his presence of mind. He pulls out a cell phone. Let us listen, "There's been an accident. I think I've killed a woman…. No, I can't remember the name of the roads at the moment….I'll leave my phone on so you can trace it….No, with any luck I'll be dead by the time you arrive." He puts the phone on the dashboard and gets out. He looks around and starts to walk away. A man runs up from the car that was trailing the one that was hit. The man tries to stop Tom. Tom shakes him off. Tom tells him, "It won't matter if I am dead." Now we watch Tom disappear into the trees.'

"The Old Man was silent now. I looked back at the accident. All I could think about was that poor young woman that Tom had killed. I felt the anger rising in me. Then I looked at the trees where Tom had disappeared. 'Where is he going?' I asked.

"'Into the wilderness,' the Old Man told me. 'It is a common destination for humans. Most enter the wilderness in only a metaphorical sense, but Tom will brave a forest at night to get there. He is really quite familiar with this area. There is a hill near here that Tom and his former wife climbed several times in the past before they were married. There was a precipice there that allowed a view of the valley. Sitting on the edge was quite an experience, the wind blowing, the valley stretched below, the excitement of risking death for that was what a slip and fall would mean. And now Tom comes to this place of beauty seeking a final end. Come, let me show this to you.'

"The next thing I know we were standing on top of a mountain looking down on the towns in the valley. 'Do you not find this beautiful?' the Old Man asked.

"I looked around. 'It's too dark. The lights in the valley are sort of cute, but it is really too dark to see anything.'

"'And still you fail to turn your eyes to the heavens. You weren't always this way. As a child, even as a young adult, you had eyes for the heavens. You saw things with such hope and wonder. Right now the greatest show awaits you and you only complain that it is too dark. It is your perception that defeats you, not the world.'

"'Don't let him get to you, kid,' I heard the Young One say. 'He tends to get like this, all mystical and the like. He doesn't understand the concerns of modern humans. There's no time to turn your eyes to the heavens when you are trying to make a living and have a little pleasure in life. He just doesn't understand us.'

"I wasn't sure if that little speech was supposed to create a bond between us, but what the Young One said had the opposite effect. I looked up at the sky and the effect was shocking. I am so used to the few stars we see in town that this just bowled me over. I started saying, 'Oh my ...,' but then I stopped before I said something inappropriate.

"The Old Man said, 'See what awaits you when you but look for it. Time has flown. I hear Tom making his way through the brush. Yes, here he is, worn out. He sits on the ground, groggy from tiredness. Now he lays down, his head on his arm, and is fast asleep. Let us look at him.'

"We walked over to where Tom lay. The Young One produced a flash. Tom's face was covered with cuts and dried blood. His hands were crusted in blood. Shirt and pants were torn and soaked with blood. The Young One said, 'Good. He has suffered. He should be ready to relieve his pain. Let me wake him up and get this done.'

"The Old Man said, 'Such determination wasted. It is sad really. His path was where there was no path. He could have stopped when a branch scraped his face or when he stumbled and fell. But he has made it here. No, I think we will allow him this sleep. Besides I think our little friend here would like to see the dawn.'

"The sky was lightening and Tom began to wake up. The Old Man turned to the Young One and said, 'Very well, it is your turn now. See what you can do to this wretched soul. We will wait over there.'

"The Old Man led me away. I looked over my shoulder to see the Young One undergo a transformation. He had worn his business clothes throughout. Suddenly he was a hiker complete with walking stick and one of those forehead lights.

"When we had moved away we turned to watch. The Young One was helping Tom up and guided him to a rock where he could sit down. I couldn't hear what they were saying. 'What will the Young One do? He won't push Tom off, will he?' I asked.

"The Old Man answered, 'No, the Young One would never do that. To have any value for him Tom must decide for himself. What the Young One will do is pretty standard. He will be solicitous of all his aches and pains while reminding him of just how awful everything has been for him. He will remind Tom of his failures, his sins. The Young One will tell Tom that his life is out of control. The decision to step off the mountain will be a chance to take control. The first step will lift the weight of life off his back. Then there's floating to earth followed by oblivion. The sweetest revenge will be on those Tom leaves behind.'

"'Will it work,' I asked. 'Will Tom throw himself off the side of the mountain?'

"The Old man said, 'The Young One is very good. He is capable of the sweetest speech. Tom will throw himself off that precipice unless he gets some help.' The Old Man turned and looked at me. 'He needs an angel,' the Old Man said. "Would you be his angel?'

"I looked at the Old Man as if he was crazy. I looked away and shook my head. 'No,' I said, 'I could never do anything like that.'

"The Old Man said, 'Then Tom will die. You are his only hope. Is it that you feel you can't or you won't? Perhaps you have judged Tom.'

"I found myself shouting at him, 'But Tom's a drunk and a womanizer.'

"Quietly the Old Man said, 'Are we talking about Jeff or Tom?'

"'But what about the woman that Tom killed?' I told him.

"'Are you sure you have all the facts?' the Old Man said. 'Or perhaps it is not Tom you are judging but me. Perhaps you have judged me over the death of the young woman and have found me wanting.'

"I turned away, looked at the ground. I started to say, 'I would never ....'

"The Old Man interrupted me. 'Yes. Yes, you would,' the Old Man said. 'Do you think I do not know? Do you think I have not heard?'

"I was ashamed. I fell on my knees and started to cry. Then the Old Man said, 'There is someone else here you have judged. I want you to forgive her.'

"I tried to say something between the sobs, but I couldn't control myself well enough to get anything out. The Old Man said, 'You, Jan, it has all been about you and not Tom. Why do you think you are here? You need to forgive yourself and give up the hate and anger that is destroying your life. When you practice killing by a thousand cuts do you really think this is any better than anything Tom may have done?'

"I was watching Tom. He was standing up looking at the edge of the cliff. The young One had his arm around his shoulder. Slowly, the Young One was moving toward the edge. The sky had lightened with the few clouds being lit by the sun just breaking the horizon.

"Suddenly, I was gripped by a fear for Tom's life. Minutes ago I would not have lifted a finger to stop Tom from committing suicide. Now I knew if Tom died a part of me would die. 'Can't you just stop Tom from going over the edge?' I asked.'

"I heard the Old Man say, 'I can do that, but I will not. If I do everything what is the value of being human. Besides, I promised the Young One that there would be no magic. Tom will have to be saved by a human heart. That is the way life works.'

"I asked him, 'What if I fail?'

"I stood up and turned around to face the Old Man. He was not there. For a second I doubted that I had ever seen him. Then I heard these words in his voice coming from inside me, 'If you fail, Tom will die. But you will not fail. I have faith in humans. Remember, fear not, you are loved.'

"I turned and looked for Tom. He had fallen on his knees and held his face in his hands. I didn't know what to do. Then I had a thought. If I could just get between him and the edge of the cliff maybe I could stop him. I ran to the edge of the cliff and looked down. It was still dark down there. That was all it was, just dark, no bottom. A chill went through me. I backed off a few feet and turned to face Tom.

"Tom dropped his hands from his face. Looking at me he asked 'Are you an angel?'

"I looked at him like he was crazy. Then I thought to turn around. The sun was just breaking through the clouds scattering rays of light with areas of gold and pink. It was an awesome display.

"When I turned back to face Tom he was getting to his feet. 'No,' I told him, 'I'm just a human. I'm here to prevent you from killing yourself.'

"Tom was only five or six feet away now. The light coming from behind me was just enough to see his face clearly. I have never seen a face look like that and never want to again. I had decided to put myself between him and the edge so that the only way he could go over the edge was to take me with him. After seeing his face I thought I was going to die.

"Tom started moving to one side and then the other trying to find a way around me. I mirrored his movements staying between him and the cliff edge. 'What do you think you are doing?' Tom asked.

"I answered him, 'I don't really know. I don't have any sweet words to talk you out of jumping off the cliff. I thought if I stay between you and the edge so the only way to make it over is to take me with you, you might reconsider.'

"Tom grabbed for me. He missed because I was diving for his ankles. I wrapped my arms around his ankles and pushed as hard as I could. Finally, Tom lost his balance and fell over backward. 'Geez, you could have killed me, us.' Tom said.

"Tom was right. We were so close to the edge that if he had fallen forward he would have gone over and taken me with him. 'I guess you weren't meant to die this way,' I told him.

"Tom tried to kick his way free, but I wasn't letting go. 'Please, let me go. Just let me go,' he said.

"I squeezed his ankles harder. 'I can't let you go. I won't let you go. If you die, I die. It is just that simple,' I told him.

"Tom's hand patted me on the head. 'You realize I could beat you until you let go,' Tom said. I flinched. 'Don't worry. I'm not going to hurt you.'

"Then Tom called out, 'God, why don't you leave me alone? Why can't I die in peace?'

"I told Tom, 'Because He can't.'

"Tom asked, 'Who can't?'

"And I told him, 'God can't leave you alone.'

"Tom said, 'He should want to.'

"I asked Tom, 'Why is that?'

"Tom said, 'I killed a woman last night.'

"I looked up at Tom from where I was wrapped around his ankles. 'We need to talk,' I said. 'I'd like to let go of your ankles so we can talk face to face. Do you think you could promise not to jump off the cliff?'

"Tom didn't say anything, but I took a chance, let go of his ankles, and grabbed his belt. 'Tell me about it,' I told him.

"Tom didn't say anything right away. I waited. At last he said, 'I hit another car with my car last night. Hit it right where the driver sits. When I got in the other car to check her she was dead, her head crushed. Now do you see? My life has been a farce. I just want to die.'

"I told him, 'So, turning your life into a tragedy would be an improvement? I don't think you know what happened. I think you've been feeling so down on yourself that you rushed to judge yourself. Let me tell you something I just learned. In the end there is only one that can judge us and that one is the source of all love. He is the reason that I am here. And He gave me a message, 'fear not, you are loved'. So, I think you need to go back and rebuild your life. No matter how hard it is, there is nothing to fear for you are loved.'

"I was quiet then. Tom didn't respond at first. Then it happened. He laughed. He threw his head back and let out a roar of a laugh. 'I am sorry. I am not laughing at you. I am not sure what I am laughing at, probably me. All I know is that I feel better. I can't explain it, really.'

"I asked him, 'So, you aren't going to kill yourself?'

"Tom answered me by saying, 'No, I am not. In fact I cannot believe I was ever going to kill myself. So, you can let me go. I promise not to do anything.'

"I let him go. We sat there in silence watching the sunrise. Finally, Tom said, 'I better head back. They are probably going to throw the book at me for leaving the scene of an accident, but at least I am alive. If I am going to make it up to that poor woman the least I can do is try to make something of my life.'

"Tom got up and started down the mountain. He had just gone a few steps when he turned to me and asked, 'Aren't you coming with me?'

"I told him, 'No. I think I have another path, but you will not be alone.'

"Tom said, 'I know that now. Even more, I feel that now.'

"Tom turned to go. After just a few steps he turned around. 'It just occurred to me. I do not know your name.'

"I told him, 'Jan.'

"Tom said, 'Thank you, Jan. Thank you for my life.'

"I watched Tom disappear into the trees. When he was gone I thought, 'And thank you, Tom, for my life.'

"That's when I woke up. I felt happy for a change. I spent all morning when I wasn't in that meeting writing down everything that I remembered about that dream so I'd have it always."

I stopped talking. Tina having finished her sandwich and soda sat across the desk from me staring. "Can I say something?" she said.

"Sure, why not."

"It's just that you were getting so bossy," Tina said. "You are one strange person."

"Yeah. Probably."

"Now, according to you in your dream this guy Tom hits a car killing the driver and then leaves the scene. How do you know it was a dream?"

"What do you mean? What else could it be?"

Tina walked around to my side of the desk and starts fooling with my computer. "Saw this article just before I came in here," Tina said.

The headline of the article read "Woman Killed, Man Hunted." I started to read and Tina read parts of it out loud. "Here we go," she said, "Dale Lewis told police 'I saw the whole thing. I was trailing her car for miles. We were doing about sixty and when she came to the stop sign she never stopped. She never even slowed down. The other guy didn't have a chance. When I got to the accident the other guy had already broken into her car and found her dead. He was dripping with blood and acting crazy saying he wanted to kill himself.' And down here John, the victim's husband, said, 'Kathy had end stage cancer. She was having such terrible pain that she was taking narcotics all the time. We had an appointment with her specialist yesterday. When I was called out of town on business she was going to reschedule. She kept the appointment anyway. I talked to her on the phone for a couple of hours after the appointment. She was pretty broken up. I told her to stay in a motel, not to drive home. Later that night I got a message on my cell. She couldn't stand the night in the hotel. She had to come home. She was in too much pain. She should never have been driving.' So, now, what do you think?"

I did not answer her right away. "Jan, you're crying. Are you okay?"

"Yeah, I think I am."

4572789

Made in the USA
Charleston, SC
11 February 2010